The Queen

The Queen

Anita Sivakumaran

To Catherine,

Best wishes.

Anita. S.

🌸 juggernaut

JUGGERNAUT BOOKS

KS House, 118 Shahpur Jat, New Delhi 110049, India

First published by Juggernaut Books 2017

ISBN 9789386228208

For sale in the Indian Subcontinent only

Typeset in Adobe Caslon Pro by R. Ajith Kumar, New Delhi

Printed at Manipal Technologies Ltd

For my daughter

Nila Whitehead

whose conception triggered the conception of this book

2005

'Turn up the AC,' said Kalai Arasi.

The thick curls on driver Ilango's head bobbed, then an icy wind enveloped her neck with a smell like the stale air from a fridge. She didn't need the AC turned up. It was January, in any case. All night the rain had fallen, heavy as rubble. Now it was a sweet, damp, cool-season Madras morning. Fresh sea winds to brace the commoners and cut-throat rich alike. But the men in the car, chosen to join her for this morning's ride to the 'fish market', as she privately referred to the lower house, were already sweating.

'OK,' she said. 'Let's go.'

Ilango gestured and four policemen leapt to swing open the gates. Even through the closed windows of the Bentley, the cacophony that greeted them as they emerged on to the street was deafening. Policemen, those guardians of majesty, twirled their moustaches and batons, shouting in gruff voices to the devotees who pushed out from the great mass to try to creep past the roadblock. All to catch a glimpse of her. One policeman lifted a skinny man in a lungi clean into the air before hurling him back into the throng. She could almost hear the policeman's thoughts: these semi-literate nincompoops, jostling as though they were in a temple to get a darshan of the goddess herself.

As though all their worries and poverty and ugliness would be swept away by a single glance from her. Kalai Arasi, Chief Minister of Tamil Nadu. No matter which gods they personally cajoled, her flesh-and-blood presence was right here – was it not? – sweeping past, no more than a flash in a window of a car worth more than their whole family could earn in a lifetime, but anyway real. Seen with their own eyes. No other flesh and blood came close, did it? Not even that beehive baba from Karnataka. And anyway, he was a Kannadiga. Kalai Arasi was one hundred per cent Tamil.

She shifted a little, the bulletproof vest beneath her sari uncomfortable as always, watching the ecstasy in the passing faces for a moment more, the thrill, the hullabaloo out there, the frothing white-clad party men, eyes not blinking for fear they might miss her passing. Then she turned her attention to the men in the car.

Manikavel, the MP for Social Affairs, was beside her. His star had been in the descendent recently. A building scam. She decided to raise it back up again. Cultivate a deep gratitude in him. He was still young. Not hardened like some . . . She would do it subtly. She was a woman, after all. And the wolves, they were all men.

'Manikavel,' she said, 'you are the best man to tell me about this poster fracas. People, you see, have been coming to me since last evening with this and that. No one says anything clearly, simply. Now you are here, I'm grateful. Guide me through this mess. Please.'

The man had another burst of sweat. Kalai Arasi's nostrils quivered. It was exasperating at times. The more she patronised them, the more they seemed to fear her. That was good. Fear was good. One feared the gods, didn't one?

Yes madam, no madam, this madam, that madam, he began, with the man in front, also sweaty – she couldn't remember his name for the moment – interjecting with his own madams. Eventually, just as they got on to Cathedral Road, Manikavel came out with the matter.

She knew it already, of course. About three dozen people had told her last night. However, no one seemed able to make up their minds (or tell her, in any case) whether it was a good thing or a bad thing, with the election now just around the corner. She turned to look out of the window, trying to decide for herself – and there they were, rows of them.

'Stop the car,' said Kalai Arasi.

Ilango, veteran, the only driver she would use, stopped the car smoothly. She opened the door herself. As she stepped out, a little clumsily, she heard a series of screeches, the cars behind hers also halting. The car in front slammed to a stop some two hundred yards ahead, and reversed at great speed. The two motorbike police U-turned and rode back. But the police jeep, the lead vehicle of her entourage, its siren blaring and lights flashing, rushed off and away into the distance.

She straightened her sari pleats. Then, with Manikavel and the other man flanking her, she approached the poster spread on the compound walls of the Agarwal Eye Hospital. There it was – the problem. Multiple images of herself, younger-looking, wearing a crown and carrying weapons with her four arms. Just like a calendar goddess. *RE-ELECT!!*, one screamed in bold ink. *Permanent CM*, announced another in swirly font. She nearly smiled, but for the fact that the two men's terrified eyes were upon her.

'Madam, look.' The other man pointed. On another part of the wall, white sari with a blue border covering her head, she was the Virgin Mary. *Holy Mother, who better?* opined this one. This time she couldn't help smiling openly. What would Sister Flavia say?

She got back into the car. She would give the matter some thought. Were the posters meant to get her votes? Would the fence-sitters be swayed? Or would they be put off? Whose brainchild were these posters? She could reward them. Or she could punish them.

Then a thought occurred to her. The Speechwriter was going to have a high old time with this. She could imagine him and his minions huffing and puffing, giving out statements to their own dailies and weeklies and sound bites to television. Blasphemy, sacrilege, bloated with hubris, etc. etc. As if she had anything to do with it.

They had barely travelled a kilometre when the car stopped again. Some fracas ahead. Several policemen approached her car. Leading them was the commissioner, gleaming brass on his lapels and belt and cap, perfectly ironed uniform, his moustache waxed stiff, his chin pointing down respectfully.

'Very sorry, madam,' he said, 'but one cannot grapple with nuns and girls.'

She peered through a gap in the khaki melee and caught

a flash of, indeed, grey-turbaned nuns and green-pinafored schoolgirls. That she should be thinking of Sister Flavia and her own school just a moment ago – and now here they all were. Her own school, though not from her own time, of course. They hadn't even changed the uniform. Same green pinafore. Same length of skirt. Same white blouse. The girls standing stiffer than army boys on an Independence Day parade.

'. . . only take a few minutes, madam,' the commissioner was saying. 'As soon as the lady police arrive, we will shift them.'

'What do they want?'

'I thought you knew, madam.' He turned panicked eyes to the men in the car.

'Tell me.'

'They are protesting the posters.'

'Don't tell me, the Virgin Mary. I see.'

They were protesting already. The nuns who kept themselves to themselves and the girls out of sight. Now arranged on the road for all to see. Such is the way of the righteous.

She opened the car door. Immediately, a hubbub started all around her. The schoolgirls, the policemen. She got out. She didn't bother checking her sari pleats. Beyond the police and the girls, behind police cordons, she could see the general public avidly watching. Then from the little gaps and side streets, autos and scooters, even with their engines switched off, strained with pure will to get on to the main road. All buzzed and whispered. She started walking. Once upon a time, she had been in school. Once she had been so young. It seemed incredible now that such a thing could be. Indeed, she had not walked on the road for what, now, years?

There they were, the nuns and girls. In rows as if at a school assembly. Sister Flavia acting as shimmy inspector. One by one, lifting up the skirts of the girls. Nasty punishments on hot days, when a demon tempted her to forgo the silly garment. Why had she ever imagined they wouldn't notice? Some girls they let pass with a wave of their hand. But Sister Flavia had an invisible antenna for girls with their shimmy-less knees quivering under their skirts. She always found them. Branded their poor bottoms. *And* sent them home to change. Now look at her. Chief Minister Kalai Arasi. Virgin Mary, indeed. Maybe Sister Flavia was still alive, and fuming at the sight of the posters. She might very well be. Old wrinkled nut with an indestructible kernel of hate.

'Madam, you cannot walk to George Town.' The commissioner was quaking in his silly boots.

Still, Sister Flavia would have the last laugh. Shawl after shawl piled on Kalai Arasi in every public outing. In such coastal weather. Plus the coat and vest. She had sworn she would do and wear as she pleased once she left school. She did too, as she pleased. In a way. For a while. Didn't she? And now, all this shawl swapping was necessary. As was the bulletproof vest. Very necessary indeed, after what happened.

'Madam?'

Kalai Arasi realised she hadn't explained to them what she was doing. She had been walking, and they were all following her, like goats. Now the nuns and girls were in front of her. Astonished at her presence. Judas or Mary.

'Madam?'

'I'll talk to them,' she said to the commissioner.

For a moment she thought it was Sister Flavia. The nun spearheading the protest. The same dimple on the cheek and the curly hair. Kalai felt sixteen so suddenly, and she hadn't felt young in such a long time, that she nearly took a step back, as a precaution, to protect herself from the nun's wrath. But no, it was not Sister Flavia. She was not sixteen.

The commissioner hung back. Kalai Arasi approached the nun close enough to notice that it was a mole, not a dimple, on her chin, that her hair was grey, not jet black, and that it was she who was trembling.

1965

Kalai was so nervous all morning there was no room for wondering why her mother looked morose. Anju had that frown on her face, that slight crinkle on the skin of her nose-stem, which meant she was being put upon by all the world, and to top it all there was a bad smell in her nostrils. In any case, Anju's moods changed quick as clouds. One minute, open-faced and smiling, the next, closed up like a book in a foreign tongue.

Anyway, Kalai had her finals results on her mind and nothing else. She hardly noticed what she ate or wore or whether the bus was empty or full. At the school gates, a classmate, her tight double plaits making her head slope like an ant's, screeched, 'Hey Kalai, you won't believe what I got.'

All the way from the school gates to the admin office, nuns and girls came up to say this and that, but Kalai's ears were filled with the sound of her own heartbeat and the words did not register.

Anju stopped outside the door and Kalai went in alone. The office staff, Prema, Gita and Subramani, broke into smiles when she entered. This wasn't unusual. Everyone knew her, of course. But when they all stood up and applauded, Kalai felt her cheeks turning hot and probably reddening. It was absolutely the best moment in the sixteen years of her life.

Outside, Sister Flavia swooped upon them and held Kalai's hand in a pincer grip as she told Anju, 'How proud you must be, Kalai's mummy. How proud the whole school is of your daughter. What a clever girl you have, Kalai's mummy.'

Kalai, mortified and blissful at the same time, absorbed the praise, with just a hint of unease at how expressionless Anju's eyes now were, how without joy, how remote.

Her best friend Pinky came and hovered behind Sister Flavia till she left. Then they giggled wordlessly at each other, shaking their heads, unable to discuss the old witch in front of Anju.

'The toilet ayahs are calling you the blessed one,' said Pinky. Pinky was an average student who would get into law college with her father's influence.

Anju mumbled something like 'Don't let this go to your head'.

'Any chance of a little celebratory tea at my house?' Pinky asked, with her eyes on Anju. Anju's remained expressionless.

'Maybe,' said Kalai, cautiously. It depended on Anju's mood.

'At least to celebrate *my* results,' laughed Pinky. 'I didn't fail a single paper.'

~

'State second, Anju. Would you believe it?' Kalai said, once she eventually saw the backs of her well-wishers at school.

Anju was busy counting the change in her handbag. They were walking to the bus stop. The air was clear and pure, the crows caw-cawed sweetly up in the trees, and the people on the road all looked friendly and lovely. She wanted to skip, but she was not a little girl any more. Anju would have a fit. As it was early afternoon, the buses whizzed past half-empty. Kalai wanted to hug her mother. But, of course, they didn't do hugs. She caught Anju's arm on the pretext of wanting to steady herself, and felt her mother's soft flesh against her thumb.

Anju pulled free from Kalai's grip and made a show of securing the handbag strap on her shoulder, her head twisted away, on the lookout for the bus.

'You don't have to be so upset, you know,' said Kalai, laughing. 'Second in the whole of Madras state is nearly as good as the first. And there is only a difference of point two per cent between the first and second, they said.'

Anju said nothing. It irritated Kalai, but only a little. Nothing would spoil this day. To top the school was all she had been expecting. She smiled at two women at the bus stop who were staring at her, envying her fairer-than-wheatish skin and big eyes and straight hair like that of a Marvadi girl. They were always staring at her beauty. Kalai would usually frown at them, but not today. She turned to Anju, who had been silently watching her, then looked away and into the distance again.

A bus came, and Anju said, 'Come on.'

'This is the wrong bus,' said Kalai. 'Doesn't take us home.'

'We are going to the beach to talk,' said Anju, and stepped up without waiting for Kalai.

~

By the time they found a rubbish-free spot just before the watermark, Kalai felt helpless against Anju's hostility. It was as if the news of her academic triumph had opened her heart to the world, only for Anju's bad humour to flood in like enemy troops.

The sea roared and crept upon Marina beach. Kalai sifted sand with her fingers while waiting for Anju to spill whatever was swilling around inside her. The dull September sun was oppressive, and the sundal-wallas were already out. A little boy appeared, holding a rusty biscuit tin propped on one shoulder and paper cones in the other hand. He looked about six or maybe eight years old. Approaching, he cried from the pit of his throat, 'Mango, coconut, fried peas sundal . . .'

'Get lost with you,' said Anju, and the boy walked off reluctantly like a piece of elastic being pulled away from them, his feet first and face last, grinning like he had been complimented.

The tide came in fast. The waves made sounds like a hard hand slapping a thigh, magnified and sent echoing through a hollow chamber.

Finally, Anju spoke. 'I have no money left.'

So it was true. Anju's acting career had ground to a halt. A minor actress, she had always played either a slutty extra with a couple of lines of dialogue, or a second comedienne. Lately, she had been trying to get some mother-of-the-hero roles. The one time she had been cast as the hero's mother, the director fired her after the first day of shooting. She did not look motherly, even with the make-up and clothes and the acting from the guts. Anju was much too saucy, and much too spirited. Her eyes flashed like a young woman's. Kalai had heard the gossip from the servants they used to have, when they didn't know she was listening.

She *was* still a young woman, her mother. Her eyes, looking out to the sea, were sad and tired, but there were no shadows under them. There was not a single grey hair on her head. She was thin. She did not have the matronly hips one wanted in a mother. She would be thirty-five in March.

'Medical fees at Ramachandra aren't that much, mummy,' said Kalai. The mummy was a slip. She had only called Anju 'mummy' as a child on the days that she ran a temperature. Anju remained silent.

'You can sell my jewels,' said Kalai. It wouldn't be a sacrifice. She liked to dress simply, in any case.

'They aren't real,' said Anju.

Kalai's throat went rigid. The waves slapped. The jewels had been a kind of insurance. They had reassured her on the days she doubted Anju's reliability.

'Well,' said Kalai, 'Stella Maris charges peanuts. I'll do a BA then. Literature or commerce. Become a secretary.'

She laughed. Of course she didn't mean that. Any second now, Anju would laugh too, and say, 'We aren't quite that desperate.'

Anju only scowled. 'No money for that either.'

'I didn't mean–' said Kalai before she realised Anju was serious. 'Come on, Anju,' she said, 'a BA costs nothing.'

'It's not just the course,' said Anju. 'We don't have any money at all.' She looked down, and then up, finally meeting Kalai's eyes.

Kalai read the hopelessness there.

'What will we do then? Must we leave home? Go elsewhere?'

'There is a solution,' said Anju, her gaze straying again. 'You could enter films.'

Kalai turned to look at the sea, digesting this. Acting. Actress. The waves broke with a sound like rocks. Those men who had recently been dropping in. 'Say hello to uncle, Kalai Arasi.' Anju usually never called her by her full name. It sounded so artificial, from her. Who were these uncouth men? Why did they run their eyes up and down her body, instead of just keeping to her face? They were sizing her up like tailors of blouses, skirts.

The noise was too much. It filled her ears, entered her head. How was she supposed to think with this ocean in front of her? Why should she be the one to supply the solution? She was only sixteen. Where was her father? He was supposed to be the provider, not her. And her brother, wasn't he responsible for the family, after her father?

'What about Ganesh?' she asked Anju. She would not cry.

'We'll have to pull him out of law college, if you won't do it.' Anju caught Kalai's hand, and caressed it. 'There is a good, decent film, baby.' Her voice had turned pleading. 'Once you finish, you can enter college. Just one year will be lost. Then you need only act in the holidays. That will keep us going.'

The sea pounded the shore, monotonous, relentless. What Kalai had meant by 'What about Ganesh?' was – why couldn't he be the provider, why does it have to be me? But he was in first year law. He had to finish. Get a decent job. Start a career. Then he could help. He couldn't very well quit now and become a clerk in some office, she knew that.

The sundal boy passed by again, then stopped in unmerited hope. 'Sister, please. No business all day.'

Kalai thought, why does he come back, after Anju dismissed him so rudely? But the boy was smarter than her, for all her coming state second. Anju was saying to him, 'Two cones. Mind that there is no sand in it.' He had more life experience, in spite of his age. He had been in the business long enough to know that people changed their minds like tides changed direction.

Expertly, the boy propped the tin between his thin knees, folded two cones and held them with one hand while filling them with the other.

Anju gave him two annas. He went away.

The tide was now retreating, the waves almost noiseless,

scuttling like crabs, just when Kalai wanted something to fill her head and drown her thoughts.

～

The summer had given way to the cool season. Kalai had been twiddling her thumbs and losing her mind with envy for all her friends who were going on to college. Finally, they were told to come to Ooty.

With two modest suitcases ('They will provide all we need,' said Anju, 'including underwear.'), they climbed into Kovai Express. For hours, Anju sat on the thin blue rexin complaining either about the slowness of the train ('Call this an express? Stopping at every two-bit town.') or about their seats ('How dare they book second-class seats for the heroine's mother and the heroine?'), while Kalai looked out of the window. The people around tried to make extra space for the unhappy, fair-skinned, well-dressed woman, and Kalai could only be amazed and embarrassed by Anju. How dark the people were, and how thin and simply dressed. How quiet and modest, unlike Anju. There was something about going out of town that made Kalai view her mother like an object in a museum.

At Coimbatore station, they got on the Nilgiri Express. Outside, the smoky blue train, named after the blue mountains, looked romantic and inviting, but inside, the second-class seats were wooden benches. Anju resolutely dragged Kalai to the first-class compartment, where she sat and glared at everybody, including the TT, who checked their tickets without comment and moved on. The people looked more well fed, and there was more room. Kalai had lost a little of her self-consciousness by then. Anju had insisted she pay attention to her looks and dress, so Kalai was wearing a new orange kameez with a pinched waist and Punjabi pyjamas that made her bottom fill out pleasingly.

The train reached Munnar station and began the slow climb up the mountain when Anju started pinning Kalai's hair up in an excruciating top bun like Sharmila Tagore's, all the time criticising Kalai's features.

'Your arms,' said Anju with a mouthful of pins, 'are at least chubby. They make up for the lack in the bosom department.'

Kalai held up a hand mirror to watch her transformation from schoolgirl to starlet. She just looked stupid.

'My face is too round for this hairstyle, Anju.'

'That's good. Tamils love a chubby face. But you have to show your modern persona. The character is also modern and educated, like you. You can't give a first impression in flat, oily hair, like a village girl.'

Kalai could only suck air in exasperation.

She knew little about her role in the movie, only that she was modern and educated. Nobody sent a script. Kalai hardly ever watched Tamil movies. She preferred Hindi movies, and the occasional Western. Her classmates would laugh if they knew she was going to be in a Tamil movie. It was not a very sophisticated thing to do. She had only told Pinky about it, but no doubt they all knew now, everyone in Madras.

Still, she had never been to Ooty. Kalai looked out of the window as they climbed the hazy blue mountain. Acres of tea leaves followed orchards of apples, people garbed in sweaters and mufflers sparsely picking their way through the hilly paths. Suddenly the train would glide past a steep drop. There was a sense of possibility and purity here, and the air was sweet. It was not so bad that the shooting should be in the hill station. She would try to find time to explore – with Anju, or maybe there were people her own age. She knew there were two more new faces in the film, a boy and a girl. The boy was older, probably eighteen, but the girl was her own age, Anju had said.

By the time the train rumbled into Ooty station, Kalai was waiting at the open door, eager to jump out. Her eyes were on a kite skimming above a little hill. She did not notice the welcome party on the platform till the train halted. When she saw them, she felt their eyes like sharp knives used to peel the skin off living things. They were a group of twenty or so men. She realised they must have been watching her, looking her up and down all along the platform as the train crawled to a halt. She drew back into the coupé. She fiddled with the luggage, leaving Anju to descend first, and only got down after the whole compartment emptied.

Anju was smiling her 'making friends' smile at an elderly man holding a garland.

'Kalai, this is the director.'

'How do you do, Mr Selveraj?' She thrust her hand at

him, only noticing too late that he was holding out his garland to her.

The men started up in malicious tones.

'Mr Selveraj?' said one. 'Call him Selveraj sir, little girl.'

Someone else said, 'That is how they speak in those convent schools.'

'Hoity-toity missy.'

Unnerved, Kalai took the garland and fussed with her handbag. Anju had bought her a new handbag, to carry make-up and money. To tip the boys. Kalai hadn't tipped anyone in her life.

'Now, now,' said Selveraj. 'Very quickly you will become accustomed to our traditions.'

So this was how it was going to be. All these men, all the time, all around.

Selveraj himself seemed inoffensive. An elderly man, he had wrinkles and a balding head, his body soft and shapeless in its baggy clothes. His gaze did not stray to her assets as he walked Anju and Kalai out of the station, then accompanied them to the hotel in his Ambassador, sitting next to his own driver with them in the back.

They drove up and down hilly streets, small and traffic-free. The driver, nevertheless, honked generously at every bend.

'Where are we staying?' asked Anju. 'What is the schedule?'

The director twisted around from the front seat. 'The starring cast, yourselves included, and some selected crew, including myself, the production manager, cameraman and dance master, will be staying at Hill Heights, a five-star hotel.'

'For the whole shoot?'

'Of course, Miss Anju.'

Pleasure radiated from Anju. A five-star hotel would compensate for the second-class tickets.

'And the schedule?'

Kalai winced. She wished Anju wouldn't overdo the haughtiness.

'Most of the movie,' he said, 'and all of the scenes involving Kalai are set in a colonial bungalow. The song-dances will be in the botanical gardens, the slopes and tea estates, all close by. It will be like a picnic.'

Anju snorted.

'I have no doubt,' said Selveraj, as the car rolled into the portico of the hotel, 'that such an intelligent and highly educated girl with such natural grace like Kalai will be a delight to work with.'

Kalai did not in the least feel reassured by the director's confidence in her as she got out of the car and climbed up the steps of the forbidding-looking hotel. The heavy, bus-wide doors were guarded by an unsmiling Nepali in a turban. Somewhat surprised that he let her pass through, she nearly stumbled on the mirror-like marble floor. A uniformed attendant plucked her handbag without ceremony. Beside her, Anju was practically singing in delight.

'How long,' Kalai asked Selveraj as they stood waiting for the lift, 'will we be here?'

'Two months,' he said.

Even a nerdy schoolgirl like Kalai knew that in movie parlance two months meant five or six. The shooting would spill into the application times for the following academic year, and she would end up losing two years instead of one. If only she were the hero, she thought, as they squeaked up in the lift, she could tell them to hurry up.

~

The next day, the movie was launched at the private grounds of the hotel. Belying the lush Ooty landscape, the grounds were barren of trees or shrubs, or even grass. Under a shamiana, a priest sat stoking a fire, and the press arrived to take pictures and write up the event. 'No interviews,' the director had told them. Only pictures.

Various photos were taken of Kalai and the director, Kalai and the hero. 'Stand close, stand close,' they exhorted her.

The only young men she knew were her brother and his few unattractive, dark friends who visited their home and never spoke to her. Her school wasn't co-ed. When Kalai did go out, she only ever went to Pinky's house, and Pinky had no brothers. Nervously she inched closer to this young, alien male whose name was Shekar. A real movie hero, in person, next to her, inches away. Flesh and blood.

She supposed Shekar was handsome. Usually, she ignored South Indian movie heroes on principle. She found attractive figures in English literature – Mr Rochester or Gatsby, and cast an occasional eye upon the Hindi movie hero who was pale-skinned, with angular features. Tamils preferred a chubby face, rounded curves, in their men and women both. Someone like her. Shekar was neither one type nor the other. Soft, but not fat, with a round, yet distinctly un-chubby face. He had curly, swept-back hair, even, bright teeth and a small, neat moustache.

She had first seen Shekar at the hotel reception that morning. Anju loudly complained to the receptionist that there was no car waiting at the steps and they weren't about to step out to look for it with all their make-up and fine clothes in such weather. Shekar descended the stairs. Look at me, she thought. No, don't look at me. He focused on the commotion surrounding Anju. He was very well dressed. The slacks and the shirt looked new, ironed, shiny smooth, and they fell from his body in a pleasing manner. He addressed Anju. Anju said something in return. He spoke a few words. Anju laughed with all her teeth. Kalai turned at the sound of thunder behind her. Anju came back to join her and the car arrived. Kalai did not ask who he was. She had to be indifferent towards the opposite sex in order to protect herself from Anju. She had noticed that he (whoever he was) was staying at the hotel. He had handed his key at the reception.

He turned out to be the Hero. A young man, a rare thing, whose path in life was crossing hers, if briefly, for a few months (two to five). Now, standing beside him, she could sense his warmth, the scent of his skin.

A photographer motioned with one hand as he adjusted focus with the other – 'closer, move closer' – and she collided with Shekar. They both offered each other startled smiles, and said something at the same time, even as the old uncle director came bustling to break it up.

'That's enough,' he said.

He turned to the photographer. 'Take some of the hero with the other heroine too.'

'Other heroine?' Kalai asked Anju. Anju stared daggers at the girl now posing with Shekar. About Kalai's age, pretty and made up, pink lipstick, pink sari, shy, posing reluctantly, becomingly, with the hero, who was exhorted to put his arm around her shoulders, and refused.

'New face,' spat Anju.

Kalai glanced at her mother, saw the anger in her eyes.

'They have brought in another girl like you, and they won't say which of you is paired with the hero, nor how big her role is. And the hero is new too. Nobody knows him in Kodambakkam.'

'It is a big director, Anju, and a big studio.'

'He was big ten years ago, not now. Yes. All the leading cast are new faces. What is he playing at?'

The hero glanced at Kalai. Or at something in her direction. He smiled. At Anju.

Anju sighed. 'Well, we must make the most of it. This is the best debut I could get for you.'

Anju gave Kalai an assessing look. 'I'll have to keep an

eye on things so they don't sideline you,' she said. 'And I'll train you to act.'

Kalai laughed. 'You will do no such thing.'

~

'Vimala, on the other hand,' said the costume witch to her assistant, 'has a splendid bosom.'

Ensconced in her den of creepy, floor-to-ceiling costumes, she fussed about with pins like a voodoo practitioner, grinding her teeth, upset over something, everything, but usually Kalai.

For four days, she'd been dressing Kalai and Vimala. She had decided in the first minute of their meeting that Kalai was the doll into whom she would stick most of her pins.

Across the room, the assistant positioned a dress on Vimala, who stood demurely, with perfect poise.

'We don't have to pad it or push it up,' continued the witch. As she spoke, her hands were busy, hoisting up Kalai's bosom in the costume she had pinned on.

They were having a final fitting before shooting began. Kalai tried her best to control her anger. Her previous outbursts had already caused everyone from the tea boy to the first assistant director to call out 'hoity-toity' or 'rude missy' whenever she passed them.

Vimala, though the same age as Kalai, had a splendid bosom. She also had a knack for pleasing everyone without even opening her mouth. Perhaps she was pleasing to everyone because she never opened her mouth. Kalai detested her. Vimala behaved as one cowed from birth. She was accompanied by her grubby, domineering uncle who never let her out of his sight, and seemed to have brought her up with the single idea of getting her into movies. He was, even then, outside the door, probably listening to every word.

'Did you never want to become anything else when you grew up?' Kalai asked the girl loudly, to drown out the costume witch's commentary about her dinky bottom.

Vimala shook her head, eyes cast down. It was as though she were already playing her role in the movie: the good, quiet and modest girl who deserved the love of the hero. They all knew the story by now and the roles they had to play. Kalai's seemed to have been designed out of spite. Not only was she mad, she also tried to steal Vimala's boyfriend. Not that she minded. Anju did. To Anju's great disappointment, gentle Vimala would play the lead. Kalai would be the 'other girl'.

Kalai thought she might as well play the other girl if she couldn't be the heroine. Both sounded equally silly, as did the story. Anju, however, was only concerned with the order of billing. Anju had hoped Kalai's name would come after the hero's, but, after much pestering, the first AD had admitted to her that Kalai would be billed at number four, after the actors who played the hero, the good heroine and the hero's father. She dared not confront the director. All Anju could do was huff and puff to Kalai.

'So this is your dream come true then, standing here,' Kalai said to Vimala. The girl was the only creature as young as herself, and who wasn't in some position of dominance over her. Even the tea boy considered Kalai beneath his contempt, by virtue of his being older, belonging to the better sex and having been in the business longer.

Vimala glanced up with a tentative smile and Kalai saw that she was terrified out of her wits. She couldn't help a feeling of satisfaction.

That good feeling didn't last long. The costume witch pushed her in front of a mirror and the sight made her aghast.

'These boobs are at my throat,' said Kalai. 'People will think kittens have crawled into my blouse.'

'You know nothing, missy, so give your mouth a rest. It is what the camera sees that is important, not what you think with your clever clever head.'

~

'Scene Three. Take Four,' Kalai heard. The clapboard sounded. She lay on a divan with her eyes closed. She tried to contain the twitching in her eyelids, her limbs. It was her first scene. She could not tell if her stomach was in her mouth or her mouth in her stomach.

'Been like this for over a year now,' her movie father said to the hero, his voice gravelly, sad notes in it like a tanpura in a concert. They were standing by her head.

'Will do my best,' said the hero. His voice conveyed the sense that he was professional, non-committal but kind, all at the same time. Gentlemanly. A prickle of desire filtered through her nerves.

'Cut,' said the director. Kalai opened her eyes. 'Stay as you are,' he said to her. Then he called to an assistant, 'Continuity, keep a watch.'

The young man in charge of continuity came to stand by Kalai's head. The director gave instructions for new camera positions, and the crew got busy.

They were in a large room. Overstuffed sofas lay in one corner. In the middle of the room, throne-like chairs surrounded a heavy, wooden table with carved gilt edges. She had earlier spied someone sticking gold paper on the back of the chairs. Crystal chandeliers above and velvet curtains on the windows. Her character was living in a movie-goer's idea of a rich person's house rather than a real rich person's house. The staircase, part of the adjoining set, had the obligatory bright red carpet.

The business end of the room was choked with crew and equipment. Kalai had no idea how the director extracted labour from the chaos of their intermingling. She closed her eyes.

She wondered what real rich people, like Pinky's family, for instance, would think of this set. While she waited for the director's call, in spite of her nervousness, she thought again of Pinky's letter and felt her eyes, still closed, prickle with tears.

Pinky had scribbled a postcard, not even bothering to write legibly. Kalai had to read it three times to make sense of it.

Dear K, what fun it must be to star in a movie! All that dancing and nice clothes too, not just fame and fortune. Do you

get to keep any clothes? I saw a pic of the new hero in Kumudam.
He's a DISH! Can you get a signed photo from him for me?
Listen, I'll write more another time. Got to dash. Going to see
–Mother India– with the hitlers and they are shouting at me
to hurry. Sorry didn't write sooner. Busy busy, classes etc. They
want me to drop contact with you. Movie heroines are prossies,
they think, and you'll corrupt my innocent mind. Bish bash.
But I promise never to forsake thee, my one true love. I'm so
j. What a squeal it must be. And me with the boring studies.
Don't forget the pic. Your dear friend, P.

Kalai missed the call to be ready. Before she knew it, the boy was yelling, 'Scene Four. Take One.' The echoing clap again.

'Action,' called the director. Fingers landed on her cheeks, and her lower eyelids were pulled down one by one. She opened her eyes and turned a leering clown face at the stranger, the hero. He sat beside her, a stethoscope around his neck, over his white coat. His hair, gelled and gleaming, overhung his forehead in the current fashion. The make-up on his face had cracked already. His lips, she noticed, were done up a shade of red to show what a dish he was in Eastman colour.

Kalai shrieked, threw off the sheet that had been covering her body and, laughing, jumped up on the bed. She put her hands on her hips, twirled and struck a pose for the camera.

This was her introduction in the movie. Behind the camera, among all the wires and equipment and pieces of prop, was a vanity mirror, and she could see herself reflected in it. Her hair hung on either side of her face in brooding plaits that emphasised her mad girl's mannerisms. She had light foundation on her cheeks, a jersey pink shade of lipstick, mascara, eyeliner and green eye shadow to indicate her difference from the good heroine and her ordered world. Her pushed-up breasts seemed to caress her throat.

She twirled round and round in front of the astonished doctor, laughing maniacally. A mad girl in a pleated western frock.

'Cut,' called the director. 'And can!'

He jumped from his high seat next to the camera and came running towards her. He seized her shoulders, and beamed like an extra spotlight.

'You, my darling girl,' he declared, 'were born for the cinema screen. You are the star of this movie.'

Kalai looked around her. The entire unit was staring at her, jaws slack. Shekar seemed genuinely unnerved. Kalai felt herself glow.

~

Scene Five. Take One. Standing on a table, the doctor and her father holding the edges so it didn't topple, Kalai disco-danced, mouthing the words to rock-and-roll music. 'The world is a mad place, I'm quite sane.'

~

Scene Six. Take One. Kalai put the stethoscope plugs in the doctor's ears and blew into the mouthpiece. He was a

second too late in reacting. There were two more takes for
him to get it right.

～

Scene Seven. Take One. Kalai twirled her puny father
around the overdecorated room, singing, 'Child is the
father of the child of the father,' in English. A sign of her
madness, the director had said to her in his briefing, was
that she spoke a lot of 'Butler English'.

～

Kalai's hair lay flat on her head, and in a single plait. Her eyes
were downcast, made up only with mascara, no eyeliner or
shadow. Her lips wore only a neutral shade of lipstick. Her
sleeves reached her elbows. Her stark white sari showed not
an inch of waist. She waited outside a closed door.

Five months and twenty-four days had passed since the
first day of shooting. They were shooting the final scenes:
seven hundred and eighty-three to seven hundred and
eighty-five.

'Action,' she heard through the door. She counted to
five under her breath, and pushed the door open. She took
three steps into the same room where her first scene had
been shot.

The hero and Vimala stood by the sofa. Their much-
fussed-over heads were turned expectantly to the closed
door. The crew were all standing behind the camera,
perfectly still.

Vimala crumpled her face and cried, 'Devi!' while the hero took a step back in silent manly shock.

Kalai gave a speech. She thanked the hero for restoring her sanity. She apologised for trying to come between the lovers. She averred that her heart and soul belonged to her dead husband. The tragic road accident on the very day of their wedding had also caused her to lose her sanity along with all memory of him. Doctor Raja, she stated with a trembling lip, was now her brother, and Kamala his perfect mate.

She joined their hands and blessed them. Her eyes sparkled with sad and happy tears both – sad for herself, happy for the lovebirds. The lovebirds exchanged ridiculous smiles like icing on the cake of their happy ending.

Then Kalai released their hands and turned to the camera to deliver the final lines of the movie.

'I will be a lonely tree from now until the end of my days on earth. My protection and my only companion shall be this white sari.'

'Cut,' said the director, his lips pursed, from his high seat next to the airborne camera. 'Put some heart into it, Kalai,' he said. 'Take Two, get ready.'

The scene was shot eighteen times. At the end of it, Kalai didn't even wait to change from the white costume, or to remove her make-up, or even to pull out the hair joints. She went straight to her room and fell on the bed, her body like a piece of rubber, her head too heavy to be held up any longer.

~

Kalai lay with a sheet drawn up to her chin, only partly awake. A joint of false hair was caught under the pillow, pulling painfully on her real hair. Her mascara-encrusted eyelashes felt like iron filings. Her eyes were gummed up and itching. She was still wearing the white sari, the symbol of tragedy, suffering and hopelessness. The symbol of a woman soiled and left by a man who was irreproachable, as he was dead. The fan rat-tat-tat-ted overhead, sending gusts of air down to comfort her. Kalai was in need of comforting. Her body ached as though someone had beaten her up. Her skin felt clammy to touch, like a yogurt pouch. Light came through the fabric of the curtains drawn over the windows. It looked like morning. She didn't feel rested one bit.

She wondered if it was better to be a spinster all her life or a widow, and whether a widow who had known love just once or maybe for a year. She did not have the experience to judge.

The bathroom latch rattled and Anju emerged. She wore a bindi, her hair was plaited and the sleeves of her blouse came halfway to her elbows.

'You are all decent,' croaked Kalai, throat like sandpaper. 'Did you run out of sleeveless blouses?'

'You don't look very well,' said Anju. She fussed with her handbag. She was always fussing with her handbag. There used to be a time, not so long ago, when she would have been seated next to Kalai, taking her temperature, stroking her forehead, forcing syrup into her mouth. Like fattening a calf.

Now the sacrifice had been made.

Kalai studied her mother. In the past weeks, she had begun noticing this look in Anju's eyes – the same look she had when calculating the weight of a basket of brinjals, not trusting the vegetable seller's scales. 'My daughter,' she kept saying to everyone, as though Kalai were an extension of her. It was as though all Kalai's glory belonged to Anju, who was too old to be anything on her own and too young to settle into dotage.

'Where are you going, Anju?'

'To this Sivan temple, along with some of the crew. Meena and Rama are coming.'

'You and a temple?'

'They were all praying, you know, when we arrived here. Promised they would offer a hundred coconuts if the shoot went well. I thought I must offer a hundred of my own if you went down well. Don't look at me like that. I'm not particularly superstitious like that, I know. But I was worried. I had to do something. Appeal to someone. I didn't know if you could act. Even you didn't know if you could act. Believe it or not, I do care about you.' She said all this scowling, as though the sight of Kalai irritated her.

'As they say, good show, mother.'

'Now get that stuff off you. It's hideous. Who on earth wears a white sari nowadays? Someone should have told the scriptwriter. You rest. I'll be back in a few hours. We might lunch at the temple. Supposed to be auspicious, eating the tamarind rice or pongal they give out as prasadam. You order room service. We will pack when I get back.'

'Back to Madras?'
'Back to Madras.'

~

Kalai was still wearing the white sari when the hero came to visit.

She had napped for an hour after Anju left. She woke up feeling better, sat up, thought about brushing her teeth, when there was a knock on the door. 'Come in,' she said, automatically, before remembering the state of her appearance.

Shekar's eyes swept over her, then he stepped in and shut the door behind him. She was exposed, cornered, but there was nothing to be done. He smiled. She realised he was shy, nervous even, and she didn't feel cornered any more. Still, she was all the more conscious of how she must look. She brushed her hair down with her hands, eyes at his knees.

'I just wanted to say hello,' he said.

She glanced up at his face.

'Hello,' she said.

He surveyed the room.

'Larger than mine,' he said.

'Yes, but it's your own room. I have to share with Anju.'

'Is she here?'

Kalai said nothing for a moment. 'No,' she said at last.

'You call your mother by her name.'

He folded his hands, looking like a schoolboy in his

brown shirt and black trousers secured high on his waist with a belt. Though filming was over, his hair was still Brylcreemed and puffed over his forehead. Now it did not look so silly to her. She didn't know why she had thought it silly in the first place. She had just been cross with everyone in the film business, she supposed. Now she wasn't so cross, maybe because she was leaving.

'I'm going back to Madras,' she said to him. 'What about you?

'To Bangalore.'

'Are you from Bangalore?'

'No. From Mysore. But I'm shooting in Bangalore. Kannada film.'

'So is this what you have always wanted? To be a movie hero?'

'Of course,' he said. 'Ever since I was three years old.'

'So did I,' she said. She didn't know why she said that. Why such a blatant lie? Was she trying to establish some sort of camaraderie with him? Was she seeking out a soulmate? All through school, there had been talk of soulmates among her friends. None of them knew what it meant, exactly. But any new girl to school they instantly liked was deemed a 'soulmate'.

'Well, no,' she said. 'I actually wanted to be a doctor, but we didn't have any money. So you see, all this is tempor–'

'I like you,' he said, and sat down on the bed abruptly, as though he'd just run up several flights of stairs and needed to catch his breath.

'Me?'

He looked at her bedcovers.

She couldn't tell if all this was some kind of a joke. Her fingers itched to smooth her hair down again. She must look like a scarecrow.

Then, he said, 'You are so . . . everyone must tell you all the time,' eyes still on her blanket.

'Tell me what?'

'That you are so beautiful.'

Kalai leapt from the bed and ran to the bathroom. Inside, she stood with her back to the door.

She called out, 'I must really get changed, you know.'

'Shall I come back in a bit?' he called back.

'Yes. No. I mean, but we are leaving tomorrow for Madras.'

'I meant later, in an hour or so.'

'I don't know. Yes. No. If you like. But what is there to talk about?'

She bit her lip. She hadn't meant to say that at all.

'OK, see you soon, perhaps.'

The 'perhaps' was mumbled, or did she imagine he said it?

Footsteps sounded very close. They paused just on the other side of the door, inches away. She held her breath. Then the front door opened and shut. He was gone.

~

For the next hour, Kalai fretted that she had scared him away by acting like an innocent. But the fretting did not stop her from showering, brushing her teeth and donning a peacock-blue churidar kameez that gave an illusion of breasts without the need for spongy pads.

Then, seated at the dressing table, she applied kohl to her eyes. She had never in her life felt this helpless, not even on that afternoon on the beach with Anju. She wished she could rewrite the scene of the hero quitting her room. She would be dressed as she was now, reclining confidently on the pristine bed. She would be looking at him through lowered lashes, saying, 'Stay. Anju won't be back for several hours.'

They would fall into each other's arms in a near swoon like Scarlett and Rhett Butler, press kisses on each other till her lips swelled. After that her imagination failed her. Glorious things would happen. Then it picked up. Marriage, happy house. He could go and be a hero. She would become a doctor and save lives. They would kiss each other goodbye at the door, after breakfast, stethoscope in her hand, a Stetson in his. They would recount their day to each other over dinner, which the servant would have cooked, not her. What if he had a mother, parents, joint family? Then they would have their private rooms upstairs, come down at mealtimes.

She was hungry. Her tummy pinched like a gossipy friend to get her attention. But she couldn't very well be stuffing her face when he turned up. The helplessness returned. She hadn't ever felt so powerless over anything. Even with Anju and this whole acting business, she was making decisions that were in her power to make. She was aware that ultimately she was choosing to do this, much as Anju put upon her. This was different. This was an emotional free fall. Within a space of minutes, the fatal minutes of her shutting herself in the bathroom and spouting nonsense and he leaving, everything was thrown in a seesaw. Everything, her emotions, her heart. She laughed aloud. It felt terrible but good.

Time passed. Frowning at the mirror didn't help. It only caked the make-up on her forehead. She didn't know what he was thinking. Had she put him off? If only he would come so she could correct it like she corrected make-up. Frown lines all smoothed and the skin peachy like Elizabeth Taylor's. She would make him see that she was, indeed, willing. That she was ripe for instruction.

Her finger was at her eye, correcting the kohl that didn't need correcting, when there was a knock on the door. Even though she had been straining her ear for precisely that knock for an entire hour, it startled her. The kohl was smudged. But there wasn't a moment. She opened the door, her lips trembling, and the director was grinning before her with his brown, corrupted teeth and a face like a stirred rain puddle.

'PKB has seen the rushes,' he gasped, 'and he wants you in his next feature.'

Kalai stared. She couldn't for a moment remember who PKB was.

'Oh, you lucky girl,' said the director. 'You lucky lucky girl.'

~

The war began the moment Anju returned from the temple and learned about PKB's interest in Kalai. The ancient director gave the impression of hopping from foot to foot in excitement and soon Anju started giving that impression too, although the emotion fuelling her was anger at Kalai's stubbornness.

'If I join college now, I'll only be a month behind, Anju,' said Kalai, racked with tears of frustration, exhaustion from the fever, and hunger. When she put her hands to her cheeks, they came away with smudges of kohl. It was as though a whole different person had been sitting in front of the mirror, making up her eyes. She was all dressed up only for this ugly argument with her mother. She sat on the bed, while the director and Anju loomed on either side, pecking at her like vultures.

'Any other girl would give her left arm to be picked by PKB,' said the director.

'Be reasonable,' said Anju. 'At least meet his people. Once he's hooked, you can ask him to film in the holidays. It's not as if I'm saying don't go to college or don't study.'

'Once he's hooked?' said Kalai. 'You don't even talk like my mother any more.'

'Yes, yes,' giggled the director. 'She looks more like your older sister, doesn't she?'

'Don't be so naive,' Kalai said to Anju. 'They won't change shoot dates to suit my convenience. I'm nobody. You promised, Anju. This one film, then I enrol in college and I think about offers only after I'm settled and have caught up with my studies. Now look at you. Back flip.'

'But this is PKB,' said Anju. 'It's like winning a lottery.'

'I don't want to play the lottery.'

'That's not the point,' said Anju. 'The point is, you've won and you want to give the money away and force your mother to become a maidservant.'

'Oh, don't be melodramatic,' snapped Kalai. 'You never had any talent for it.'

That shut Anju up. She went off with the director to conspire somewhere and only came back at bedtime. She didn't speak a word. The silent treatment continued the next day on the train back to Madras.

～

Pinky's watchman opened the gates for Kalai, nodding and smiling.

'Go in, baby. They are in the house.'

Pinky's house lay at the end of a long, secluded drive lined on either side with creepers and trees that reached up and overhung. Entering it was to leave the city behind. She always fancied it was somewhat like entering a fairy tale. She, who had never lived anywhere but in the brick-and-steel city, wanted to live like this in a house of treats in a fairy forest. The noise of the city had been left at the gates. A peace and silence hugged the large house. There were more rooms than people. No one jostled for access to the bathroom. Buckets of washing were not thrust in the queue.

Kalai rested her hand for a moment on the heavy wooden door. Rosewood. She braced herself as she pushed the door open. The two Labradors didn't bound towards her as usual, didn't knock her down with their paws on her shoulders. Where were they? Where was everyone?

She wandered in, calling out, 'Hello . . .' No one answered.

She took the precious, unsupervised minutes to gorge her eyes on everything she coveted. The expensive and comfortable sofas and divans, the teak swing at the back of the main hall, the cane patio chairs. The dark TV den. The guest washroom with its rose-stone sink, so clean you could sleep in it. Pinky's parents' bedroom suite, its dressing room with the walk-in closet, the great sunken bath. She noted the changes, memorised new positions, additions. She made a mental catalogue.

She reached the dogs' room. Yes, the dogs had their own room and ceiling fan. No dogs. Where was everyone? Three servants, the gardener and his assistant, the rota of watchmen who all hurried to open the gates when cars beeped impatiently. The polite driver who never spoke a word. Where were Pinky's parents, whom she coveted above even the house, they who showered such kindness on the poor, fatherless girl.

She found Pinky's mother in one of the ground-floor bedrooms. She sat on a sea-size bed, reading and humming to herself, her leg in a cast.

'Hello, aunty,' said Kalai. 'How are you? What happened to your leg?'

'Kalai, when did you get back? It's my arthritis. For the swelling to go down.'

There were grey circles under her eyes. She looked haggard, and seemed in such pain she couldn't give Kalai her usual smile, only a grimace. Still, Kalai had expected a torrent of questions. But Pinky's mother said nothing. Kalai became aware that she might be intruding. Pinky's mother laid the little weekly down and joined her hands on her lap.

'When did you get back?'

'Just an hour ago.'

Pinky's mother seemed to be looking at Kalai in a strange way, her eyes remarkably like her dogs' as they came bounding through the driveway and launched themselves on her chest. It seemed as if she was considering the words she had on the tip of her tongue. Kalai decided she didn't want to hear them.

'Where is Pinky, aunty?'

'Upstairs.'

The staircase was beautiful, minimalist. A sliver of a hand rail. Each stair stabbed into the wall. Kalai padded up, luxuriating in the feel of the cool grey stone. She had no idea what kind of stone, something expensive and rare and brought from far away. The stairwell was high with a stained-glass skylight. It occurred to her that the cubic space of her and Anju's home was less than the cubic space of this stairwell.

When she had come to Pinky's house for the first time, her father had asked where she lived. She'd said, 'Just the next street, uncle. A portion in number eighty-eight.'

'That house next to the cowsheds?' he said. 'The one that

used to be Mudaliar's. Then he sold it to some cowpoke, and he's mangled it into all these rabbit warren portions. Can humans live there? And the whole street is filled with cow dung. Your father should have had a word about it. The cowpoke should clean up the mess.'

Kalai had been flattered that such a good, important man should have strong emotions for her state of affairs. That he should have opinions at all of her life and housing situation. She had said, 'Yes, uncle,' quite happily, not even thinking to inform him that her father was no longer in the picture.

His comments, nevertheless, had made her aware of how limited her experiences were, how narrow the view from her window. She and Anju (Ganesh was leaving for college) had moved to the portion from a bedsit, and Kalai had been luxuriating in the extra room. Two rooms for two people had seemed enough for her. One living, one bed. The kitchen in the corner of the living room. The bathroom and toilet outside, communal.

Of course, there were things like hygiene to consider, as Pinky's father had pointed out. He was what she had imagined a father ought to be. Rich, important, full of opinions, yet kind, ready to give hugs. He was the only man she had ever hugged. And after Pinky, the only person. Pinky's mother was a little more traditional. Anju did not even touch Kalai, except to slap her now and then to correct her attitude or teach her a lesson.

Upstairs, Pinky's bedroom was locked. Kalai called out. There was no answer. She put her ear on the door, heard the muffled thud of music. She rattled the knob. There was no answer. She thumped her fist on the door. Nearly a minute later, it opened.

'Oh, *Kalli*,' exclaimed the skinny, pristine Pinky, shouting over the music. She hugged Kalai. 'Oh, it's so good to see you. Come.'

Kalai sprawled on Pinky's queen-size bed and breathed in the fragrance of the bedcovers. They used some special washing powder. She drew a pillow (so plump, so soft) to her and curled around it. She felt the coils of tension fall from her, and closed her eyes. She could relax like this only here, never in her own home.

The music thumped.

'Turn it down,' she said to Pinky. 'There is so much to talk about.'

Pinky lifted the arm of the record player and the Beatles ceased their happy lament.

'Did you see my mother?' she asked. There was something in her tone of voice, a warning.

'Yes. Not very talkative. She looks ill.'

'She is always ill,' said Pinky. She laughed, an artificial sound. 'But I've been waiting to hear all about your adventures. Tell me everything. Did you get the photo?'

It was just like Pinky to be mercenary, to get to the point quickly, to seize on what mattered to her. Kalai turned her nose into the pillow, and breathed in the fragrance again. Then, turning around, dismissing her irritation, she fished out the photo to whoops of joy. When they got tired of inspecting the photo, Kalai poured out a summary of events.

She told Pinky about the score of men turning up at the station to garland her, the costume lady's jibes about her gooseberry breasts, the ridiculous songs and dances she had to do in the character of the mad girl and the silly speech at the end. She even told Pinky about the hero turning up at her hotel room, shy and nervous like a new bridegroom, confessing that he liked her, sitting so close on her bed while she lay there looking like a scarecrow, and how she had run into the bathroom in a panic.

Telling it all to Pinky, it sounded like a story from a book, a very funny story. Pinky rolled about on the bed, squealing, 'Oh God, oh no,' splitting herself with giggles. The only details Kalai left out were Anju's transformation into this crowing, siren mother, her hard eyes and cutting words, and Kalai's unease and suffering through all the incidents that sounded so funny in the telling. She also left out her despair at the uncertainty that Shekar would ever look her up in Madras.

'I'm so jealous,' said Pinky, sitting up. 'I'd give anything to have him tell me *he liked me*.'

'But then what will you do? You can't very well marry him, can you?'

'Marry? My parents would have a fit. They think actors are . . .'

'Are what?'

'It's nothing personal.'

'Do they have a problem with me now?'

'It isn't as though you are going back to it, are you? You are enrolling in college. Hopefully your film will flop and nobody will take notice of it, and life will be back to normal again. Don't worry.'

'I'm not worried,' said Kalai.

'Can't blame them. They don't know your mother pushed you into it.'

It seemed unfair that Pinky's parents would make a judgement about her without even finding out what she thought about the acting business, and whether she had submitted to it willingly. And Pinky hadn't defended her, laid out the circumstances to them. If she had, Pinky would be telling her all about it, to earn brownie points. *Oh, what a good friend I am to you. Going against my parents just for your sake.*

But then Kalai remembered, they were too rich to take someone like her that seriously, and it probably never came to any discussion at all. Even to Pinky, she wasn't important enough to defend. A rich girl had a lot of friends.

'You don't have a problem with this acting business, do you?' said Kalai. 'Just for clarification.'

'Not at all. Are you joking? I'd switch places with you in a heartbeat.'

'What will you do if I continue acting?' She felt like testing Pinky's friendship.

'But you don't want to.'

'What if I do?'

Pinky looked away, frowning. 'My parents won't allow me to be friends with you any more.'

'You won't defy them?'

'I could try, but it will be such a pain. Where will we meet?'

'Outside? My house?'

'They will kill me if they found out. And I will develop a bad reputation if people see me outside too much.'

'So you will cut your friendship if your parents reject me.'

'You are harsh. What am I supposed to do? Walk out of my house for your sake?'

'Where is the loyalty to your best friend?'

'What you suggest isn't practical.' Pinky's face went red, as though she was about to cry. 'What happened to you, anyway? Why are you making up extreme, perverse scenarios?'

'It's the principle of the thing,' mumbled Kalai. But she was now chastened. 'I'm sorry,' she said. 'Anju has been driving me crazy. You are right. I'm just going to join college, and we will be as before, thank goodness.'

~

Kalai slipped out of Pinky's house without saying goodbye to her mother. Dusk had fallen, and with it came the fragrance of the evening jasmine. She heard the dogs prowling in the garden. A maid was scrubbing a big, round vessel in a corner, near the garage. Her hand clenched coconut fibre that went over the aluminium like a saw. Kalai's ears tingled. The maid, immersed in her task, did not see Kalai.

She walked through the garden adjoining the driveway. There was a path that led to the front gate. It was like walking through the night forest. The foliage hung darkly in sympathy. Cicadas racketed. She pretended it wasn't Pinky's garden. She asked herself questions and answered them. Oh, where am I? I'm utterly lost in a forest, and there's no one around. Who are your parents? I'm an orphan. Who are your friends? No one.

Her heart seemed to lift up in her ribcage. Muscles in her stomach relaxed. She could walk here forever, her face in the darkness so no one could tell who she was. But there was the gate. The end of the forest. Back into the city. Her insides contracted again and the heart sank back to its accustomed place.

The watchman had a kindly, wrinkled face. He said, 'See you again, baby. Walk home carefully.'

Kalai nearly broke then. She wanted to go crying into his arms, stain his khaki breast with her tears so he could whisper, 'There, there,' and pat her on the shoulder. Like a grandfather would.

A car slowed in the dusk near the gate, and she thought Pinky's father had come home, and was pleased, before it sped away, and she remembered that he disapproved of her too. She thought of his hugs, which she would not get any more. The watchman was looking at her, still smiling, expectant, as though she was going to say something.

'Thank you, grandpa,' she said to him. 'I'll see you soon.'

The watchman waved to her, pleased to have been addressed as grandpa by a rich and superior girl like her.

~

Kalai walked home. The varying dullness and the sharpness of things around her, the flaking tar, the stones, the holes, the men who constantly trespassed into her private circumference to make themselves alive in her eyes, they exhausted her. They battered at her like waves on the shore. She tried to recapture the wonderful hour in Ooty when, giddy with fever and anticipation, glowing like a paper lantern, she had cleaned and decorated herself for the hero's arrival.

She could not remember clearly any more how it had felt. The first flush of love. She was now old beyond her years and that short hour was already in the distant, inaccessible past.

Clumps of people stood here and there on her street. There was the hush of awe that usually accompanied bad news. Or was it the anticipation of something momentous, like the descending of God upon someone's head in a temple festival?

A good crowd milled at her gate. People stared at her as she walked by, but they didn't know her, and they did not seem particularly interested in her. She was just some convent-school girl. *White Sari* was still on the editing table.

She climbed the narrow stairs, cheaply made and

crumbling, only a foot and a half wide, attached to the side of the house like an afterthought. There were men standing on the stairs. They moved up or down, letting her pass without touching her. She felt covert eyes on her, calculating, assessing. There were one or two intakes of breath. A man with sparkling eyes opened his mouth to speak, but she swept her gaze away from him, and he held his tongue.

The trail of people, like breadcrumbs, led to her front door. Anju is dead, she thought. There was fear. Relief. She would weep for her mother. She would now be an orphan. Was there insurance? She and Ganesh would split it equally. Perhaps Pinky's parents would adopt her. Or she would live on her own with a maid to cook and clean while she went to college. He would hear. He would come. Freedom, love, registered marriage. Pictures of Anju on the wall, looking demure in blouses with sleeves. Fair-skinned grandchildren.

It could not be. That was too easy, she thought, pushing open the door, and, of course, there Anju was, present like a grindstone, eyes wide with news. Kalai's stomach flip-flopped. Ganesh was dead. Now it was truly just her and Anju, locked in a stranglehold. He would not now ever get a job and release her.

Who was on their sagging tea couch? A man in a veshti and shirt so white and bright it hurt the eyes. A scarf with two bold stripes of black and gold on his shoulder. A politician. There was no one else in the flat.

No. It wasn't a politician. He lifted his face at her

approach and smiled. Eyes hard and black and intelligent and full of mirth. What did they say about his features? 'A divine grace hangs upon them.' Silly thing to say. But she saw that the hyperbole was, in its way, justified. It was as though there was nobody else in the world. He was the only star in the sky. The star of Tamil cinema. The other heroes mere children.

'Here she is,' announced Anju, then retreated to a corner, and stayed invisible.

He made forests and rivers switch places with a nod of his head. He was the man who was going to tell the people of Madras state who to vote for in the next elections. He was, they said, entering politics, to put his superpowers to altruistic use.

She had heard or read his name every day of her life. He was a complete stranger, and yet as familiar as a household god.

PKB smiled briskly. 'Arasi,' he said, as though he had known her always, 'I want you to be my queen.'

~

With a papier mâché crown atop her Sharmila Tagore hairdo, the queen sat on a gilt throne, surveying all. Her gaze, imperious, impervious, lit by the arrogance of virgin youth, swept slowly from left to right. It was a gaze that had never met its equal or superior (it would, in due course, of the movie, meet PKB). It swept, for the moment unchallenged, from right to left, till the director shouted, 'Cut.'

Kalai was helped from the throne by two girls. As she walked the short distance to the green room, they carried her train and various shawls. How quickly everything can change, she thought, as she gave herself over to the hair and make-up assistants. She was the heroine of not just any movie, but the most anticipated in Tamil cinema history. *People's Champion* was set to launch PKB's political career, according to the buzz in the movie magazines and among the crew.

The hairdresser began pulling beaded pins from her hair. An assistant handed her a magazine. She was on the cover, looking demure. A still from the publicity shoot around the time of the launch. The magazine would have been happy with a still from *White Sari*, but there were no stills from that film of her looking demure. She flipped to the page where there was a write-up about her. By then, every weekly had done a profile. The same summary. Clever, modern, arrogant. Spectacular talent. It was part truth, part exaggeration. She was neither that clever nor that arrogant. Her talent only stood out because it was a world of ham actors with four fixed expressions.

Whispers and tinkling at the doorway. Her gofer poked his nervous head around the door. 'Some ladies for your autograph, madam. Ravi sir sent them.'

'Send them in,' she said, closed the magazine and turned it over in her lap. What would they think, her admiring her own photo in a magazine? Anju would have the correct comment to puncture her ego.

They came in. College girls with movie-producer

fathers, giggling as she signed. They couldn't speak for shyness.

'Good luck,' she said, handing the notebooks back. Good luck, generally. For your studies. For your life. She frowned after them. The hairdresser apologised for pulling too hard.

She noticed their new heels as they walked out. Their bags. Their churidars. 'You are taking forever,' she said to the hairdresser. She would go shopping, get something stylish herself.

She opened the magazine again and looked at the advertisements. Saris, detergents, pain balms. Shopping was a recent habit, already ingrained in their routines. Like brushing their hair or teeth. Anju waited for Kalai to come home so they could go shopping. They would go in their new car, an Ambassador. They still didn't have the nerve (nor yet the money) for anything fancier. Even though she was the single female lead, her call sheet was only twenty half-days. She was in one-fourth or fewer of the total scenes. Plenty of time for shopping. Her schedule was fitted around PKB's, who was shooting forty-five twelve-hour days.

They had many things to buy, for themselves, to make up for the years of austerity, and also for the new house. Four rooms. In a road that didn't flood in the monsoon season. In Alwarpet. They hadn't even signed the papers, and already Anju worried it was too small. 'Too small for what?' Kalai had asked her. It was only the two of them. Kalai had asked Ganesh if he wanted to stay with them, now that they had a big house, but he said he preferred sharing a hostel room. They had a bedroom, a parlour, a dining room and a kitchen. They bought a Tetron transistor to put in the parlour.

In the mirror, where the hairdresser was still pulling out the pins, she saw Ilango approach, holding a drink as though he were holding a live puppy.

'Apple juice, baby,' said Ilango, shoulders crooking in deference. Her personal gofer, at her beck and call twenty-four seven till the shooting finished.

'Put it down, Ilango,' she said, 'and please call me Kalai, not baby.'

Ilango nodded away in an exaggerated fashion, so she knew he wouldn't comply.

'Shouldn't I already be on set? Why is this taking so long?' She raised exasperated eyes to the hairdresser in the mirror.

'Last pin, madam,' he said.

They couldn't make up their minds, any of them, whether to call her baby or madam.

Sipping her apple juice in the green room, Ilango watching anxiously from his stool so she wouldn't have to hold the glass a second after finishing the juice, Kalai allowed the hairdresser to redo her hair in a less regal, loose and romantic fashion.

The hairdresser kept looking at the clock on the wall. His fingers shook. In precisely ten minutes, they would start shooting a scene involving Kalai and PKB. PKB arrived on the dot for his scenes, completed them in one or, owing to a mistake by a co-star, two takes, and left the set the minute the director called, 'Cut.'

PKB had his own make-up man, hairstylist and a gofer on permanent employ. He also had a manager, a secretary and someone known as a publicist. He had costumes delivered to his house or rooms, and arrived at the shoot completely dressed and in character. Or, as the critics said, he arrived to play himself. Or, as the cynics said, he arrived to play the persona he wanted to play – the inimitable, lovable, intelligent, strong, mother-loving beloved of the poor. No matter how the individual roles and storylines differed, no matter how extraordinary the costumes were, they said PKB played the same character. In his last movie, a blockbuster, he had been a pirate in a sleeveless jacket, jodhpurs, leather boots and a conical hat. In this movie, he dressed like Hamlet on a London stage. He was also, always, PKB, and it was PKB people went to see in the movies, not the pirate or the prince.

The hair was done. Kalai's tresses, bulked up with a wig, curled and twirled down either side of her face. She was still in her 'imperial' queen costume, minus the train. She took a last sip of the juice. The glass was snatched away.

'Give me my costume for the next scene,' she told Ilango.

Instead of leaping to the task, he stood there fidgeting.

'Where's the costume?'

Ilango's eyes flicked towards the adjoining room. She could hear sounds of frustration emerging from it. She went in. The costumer sat at a sewing machine, struggling to pin pleats together on a diaphanous white sari-maxi, which was a pure Tamil cinema invention, and never seen outside a movie screen. They were running late.

'What will I do?' moaned the costumer. 'Director sir will remove my entrails.'

He was squeezing the pleats with safety pins. He stabbed his fingers, then bounced around trying to keep from staining the white sari.

'Why isn't it ready?' asked Kalai.

'I had the blue sari all ready. But PKB sir's man phoned just before he left home and said that sir had a change of mind about his costume and was going to wear rose and black. And he wanted you to wear white. I'll need at least twenty minutes.'

Kalai stood up. 'You slow down and do it properly. I'll go and tell the director it will take time.'

'Bless you, baby,' said the costumer. 'I mean, madam. Sorry, madam.'

Kalai smiled. 'You can call me baby, Mr Hanifa,' she said. 'I'll be back soon. Don't worry.'

~

The set was hushed. Crew tiptoed nervously, readying and re-readying things. The director was across the floor, turned away from her. Between them lay an elaborate lounge with lots of couches and a round, revolving bed. She could see the director's head above his chair, almost entirely obscured by the enormous Stetson he liked to wear.

The director and PKB sat side by side in chairs bearing

the labels DIRECTOR and PKB. Kalai approached, and her eyes turned from the one to the other. Some instinct made her address her co-star rather than the director. Perhaps it was the way they sat, the director nervous, shrinking under his Stetson, while PKB was relaxed, ankles crossed and lightly jiggling up and down.

'Mr PKB,' said Kalai, 'it looks like the costume will take twenty more minutes. It is not the costumer's fault, nor mine.'

She knew that if she had been this forward at the set of *White Sari* her career would have crashed as instantly as a bridge in a World War II movie. But as the 'chosen' heroine of PKB, she could be forward.

All he had said was, 'I want you to be my queen,' and she'd said, 'Of course, Mr PKB.' He had smiled and left. She had stood around as if a ghost had slapped her while Anju jumped around in joy, even very nearly hugging Kalai. Only then had she realised that she'd said yes to being in another movie.

Since then, she'd only seen him with his full film gear on, as now. He wore a frothy wig that bulged over his forehead like ice cream over its cone. His cheeks were rose-dusted and his eyes lined with kohl. He wore pale red lipstick. His costume hurt the eye. Black shirt with fashionably short, folded sleeves, a deep-rose tapering trousers modelled on Montgomery Clift's, with extra pleats and loops at the waist, but no belt.

She knew his shoes were Italian, sent by special order from Milan. She knew by now that even though he looked ridiculous in person, he looked great on screen, and that the people would once again swoon at the sight of him.

PKB smiled the smile that devastated the hearts of millions of Tamil mothers, including Anju, and said to her in English, 'Miss Arasi, it's not a problem. We will wait for you.'

~

Kalai lay on the revolving bed singing a romantic song, fantasising about PKB. To keep it all family friendly, the lyrics only held bare insinuations of sex. She danced around the room, pursing her lips, batting her eyelids and hugging herself. And at certain points in the song, when the voice of the playback singer hit a high note that led to a violin crescendo, she clutched an overstuffed pillow and writhed on the bed. They shot several variations on the theme, in different parts of the room. She leaned and breathed heavily on the armchair, piano, sofa, wallpaper. Then they prepared to shoot the parts of the song in which PKB himself appeared, as though in her fevered imagination.

Contact between them was minimal. First he stood by the door, smiling and watching as she twirled about the room singing and gasping. Then, as she lay on the bed and revolved with her eyes closed, he stood bending over her, admiring her expressions of ecstasy. She then twirled around him and, as she came near him, he tried to grab her, but always she slipped away, blushing and laughing.

Finally, towards the end of the song, he succeeded in

grabbing her. He bent her over his arm as she sang, gazing into his eyes. She felt a kind of vertigo. He allowed her to straighten and, as she continued singing with her eyes locked with his, he picked her up. Kalai felt the strength of his arms as he carried her to the revolving bed and laid her on it. He lay next to her, ran his hand up and down her arms as though she were a bolt of silk. She felt herself drawn to him. It seemed natural to be singing this song of insinuation. It didn't seem silly at all, this extreme yet chaste eroticism. Of course, it was supposed to be her character's fantasy. They would never behave like this in real life. But she was the actress living out a fantasy for the viewing public. Even though it was in her dream that PKB was breathing upon her face and holding her so close she could see the whites of his eyes, and none of it was supposed to be real, yet it was all real, and she was physically experiencing it. Her heart ran away from her body. Her breath threatened to desert her. Then, with his head to the camera, hiding her face, he bent closer, and moved his neck as if he was kissing her. On this shot the lights were dimmed.

PKB's lips hovered a centimetre from hers. Like a child helplessly reaching for the moon that hung from the bars of a window, her lips reached his. His red lipstick blended into her red lipstick for one long second. Then the lights came back on and the director shouted, 'Cut.'

She saw PKB leave the set without a word to anyone. An assistant thrust a giant pillow into her hands as she lay in the same position, dishevelled, frustrated, and extremely self-conscious. But nobody had noticed anything. The crew ran around setting up for the next shot. The director instructed the cameraman. Only her gofer stood next to her chair, smiling at her in a knowing way. She blinked at him, wondering. Then the first AD called, 'Standby.'

The lights darkened. As they began to brighten once more, Kalai writhed on the bed with the giant cushion, and the final few seconds of music played. She opened her eyes, noticed that she was holding a pillow and not PKB. She blushed and smiled, then buried her face in the pillow's fat comfort to the jangle of the final notes of an electric guitar.

~

Anju and Kalai arrived in Mahabalipuram in their new car. They wore Benares silk saris and their hair frothed and curved up above their heads in Hindi film fashion. Kalai was shooting the fishing village scenes. Seated beside her in the back seat of the Ambassador, Anju already carried about her like a shawl the air of nonchalance that rich people who were pampered by servants possessed. Kalai, too, was beginning to take it for granted that people who found it their duty to serve their every whim would do things for them just to their liking. They got out of the car and passed like ice cream cones through doors that were opened for them. The bags would be taken care of by invisible, efficient hands.

PKB, Kalai and the director were to stay overnight in the five-star resort. The rest of the small crew lodged in a cheap guest house, six or ten to a room.

As they strolled through the lobby, it amazed Kalai how swiftly they had become familiar with this game, even though this was the first time they had ever been anywhere as grand as this resort. Kalai, behind her sunglasses, could stare as much as she liked. Anju, insulated as she was by the honour of being the heroine's mother, also stared, though she wore no sunglasses.

The lobby was covered floor to ceiling in carpets and tapestries. Shimmering satin curtains fanned over the tall windows. Flower arrangements as big as elephant heads stood here and there. Old oils of maharajas and ranis hung on the walls, painted in colours Kalai had never seen before. And to top it all, there was a huge marble fountain gushing in the middle of the lobby. She walked over to it while Anju and her gofer approached the receptionist. A naked marble nymph with pomegranate breasts poured a stream of water from her mouth. It gurgled down to the basin below where goldfish swam.

They got into a brass-and-mirror-lined elevator that tinkled Western classical music from hidden speakers. The bellboy, putting the key in the door, informed them in hushed tones that their room was right next to PKB's. For this, Anju tipped him extra, though she did so with a sour face. Then, before the bellboy turned to go, with Anju gazing into the bathroom, Kalai slipped a big, crisp note into his hand. She laughed silently at his expression.

~

In a hut by the beach, under a swaying coconut tree, the prince, in the guise of a fisherman, spoke in stage whispers with his lieutenant, also in disguise. Holding sticks, they drew lines on the sand floor. They were planning an insurrection against the usurpers of the throne.

'It is a dangerous mission,' said the lieutenant.

'We will, in all probability, die,' said the prince.

'It is worthwhile to die defending our motherland,' said the lieutenant.

'Bravo,' said the prince. He praised the lieutenant's patriotism and declared to the camera that if he could also give his life for the motherland he would die with a smile on his face. For who knew what was in store?

They looked at each other with grim, fatalistic faces. The queen, who had been listening at the door, in the guise of a fisherwoman, rushed in. She fell to her knees sobbing in front of the prince.

'Do not embark on such a dangerous mission, I beg you.' Kalai clutched PKB's legs.

'How could I stand by,' said PKB, 'and watch my people suffer tyranny under an evil usurper?'

He held Kalai by the shoulders, drew her up. Tears streamed down both their faces.

'I have to do this,' he said.

The lieutenant stood to one side, face averted to give them privacy. The director had instructed him that when Kalai appeared he was to keep an expression like mustard seeds were spluttering in his face, like they spluttered in hot oil. He had to express his dislike for the queen without using words.

'My army is yours,' said Kalai. 'Take my experienced generals and go to war from my side of the border. Victory, then, is yours. As you know, my army is unparalleled in strength.'

At that, PKB released her shoulders and declared, 'I do not need a foreigner's army. I have millions of the poor whose hearts I have captured.'

Then, instead of continuing the speech to the camera, he pursed his lips.

'Cut,' yelled the director. 'What is it, PKB sir?'

'I don't like this line. It doesn't sound right.'

'But we need the line to advance the plot. Shall I send for the scriptwriter? We can shoot tomorrow.'

'No need. We'll work it out ourselves. It's only this one line. How else can I say it?'

Everyone stood around blankly. Kalai was still on the floor, kneeling, glycerine tears wetting her cheeks. She got up and went to her chair, which had HEROINE stuck to its back. From there, she watched them discuss the troubling line of dialogue.

'We've got to put in the bit about patriotism and not needing a foreigner's army when the people are enough to fight an evil tyrant,' said the director. 'Or the story cannot advance.'

He seemed ever so slightly petulant. Kalai wondered how much of the story was actually his idea. She also wondered if he would direct another movie for PKB.

She could not read PKB's expressions. His thoughts were well hidden behind that pancake make-up covering his wrinkles. Not that she remembered if he even had wrinkles. His appearance in her flat was now a blank to her. She remembered the force of his presence, but none of his features. Now it felt queer to be wondering what he looked like without the make-up and the wig. Did he wonder about her too?

PKB was saying, 'How could one put it without sounding rude? I can't call my own beloved a foreigner. Can we not be more elegant?'

He had glanced her way when he said 'my own beloved'. Kalai felt the full force of his eyes.

The director said, 'We cannot be too subtle with the dialogue or the people won't understand it. Bear in mind your audience base is mostly illiterate peasants. We've got to keep it simple, keep it black and white.' He paused, then added in a different tone of voice, 'It's what Mr Mani emphasised.'

Mr Mani was PKB's publicist. Kalai had not known what a publicist was until she met him. He would suddenly appear, go over the script, lock heads with the writer. He would give the impression of nibbling, like a rat, at the ear of the director, whose face would grow cloudy and eyebrows twist till he left. She still wasn't clear exactly what Mr Mani did. Even Anju was baffled by the man. He was foreign-educated, dressed in jeans, sneered a lot, drank like a fish, smoked like a chimney. Whispers among the crew suggested he was secretly teaching PKB English. Her gofer had said waspishly, 'What else could he usefully do?'

PKB was frowning, the director was frowning and

behind them, having contributed not a single word to the conversation so far, the lieutenant, nevertheless, was frowning.

The solution was so simple, so obvious, that Kalai laughed, a sound like the clapboard. She jumped up from her chair and ran to them.

'Mr PKB,' she said, 'there is a perfect compromise.'

'Oh, not now, Miss Kalai,' grumbled the director.

Kalai felt her smile stiffen.

'Tell me, Miss Arasi,' said PKB. 'What should we do?'

'You see,' she said, now only half-heartedly, 'you don't have to change that line even a little bit. Just have your lieutenant say it.'

PKB beamed. He patted her shoulder.

So the lieutenant said it, and it was as though he was speaking on behalf of the million peasants. PKB remained the prince with much superior sensibilities, who could never be so rude to a woman, especially his beloved. He shushed and reprimanded the lieutenant for his rudeness to the queen. But the pertinent thing was said. The plot was advanced.

The next day they began shooting a sad song where the prince and the queen said goodbye to each other. Goodbye, till we meet again, goodbye. They held each other's cheeks, gazed into each other's eyes, and Kalai could barely mouth the words, what with her fingers itching to pull away his wig, wipe away his make-up, unmask the juggernaut.

From the moment her lips touched PKB's upon the revolving bed, with nearly a hundred people watching them, but not seeing a thing in the dark, Kalai plunged into an emotional turmoil. She had never touched lips with anyone before. It wasn't something a girl did. And she most certainly had never imagined she would initiate such a thing herself. She was sure the gofer suspected something. And PKB, obviously, felt her lips on his.

She paced about the flat, agitated, not noticing the food on her plate, not hearing the transistor tuned to Ceylon station, not noticing Anju giving her appraising looks. Then, suddenly, the radio was turned off and Anju held her wrist like a crab might.

'Virginity,' she said, 'is the only way to ensure an actress's longevity.'

Kalai blanched, afraid and embarrassed in equal measure. How did Anju know what she was thinking? Why was she using words one ought to never use with one's family? Kalai wanted to close her ears.

'Don't you ever forget,' hissed Anju, 'that they will toss you out like sugarcane husk once they extract all the juice from you. Be yourself. Do you understand me? Remain yourself. Guard it like a treasure.'

'Oh, do shut up, Anju,' said Kalai. She could not bear to hear any more. Anju did not even like to refer to her periods. When she was fourteen, Kalai had gone for a whole day in school letting the blood stain her skirt, not understanding what was happening, and what she ought to do. Nobody called attention to the back of her skirt, where the wetness was spreading, brown on the light green, till a classmate grabbed her arm and pulled her to the toilet. She thrust a pad into her hands, instructed her hatefully on what to do. Kalai went home, still in the same disgusting skirt. She found Anju scrubbing a pot in the kitchen. By then, they could not afford any help at home. Kalai said, her voice sounding broken even to her, 'Anju, look,' and pulled the skirt around to show her.

Anju only said, 'Take those clothes off and wash them. I'll get you some rags.'

Here she was, now, putting voice to things that were only ever insinuated third hand. To speak directly about them was shame, shame, shame.

Kalai, once the shock had passed, felt a slow fuse of anger flare. 'How could she?' she found herself saying aloud when there was no one around. How could she? How could she? Give me one chance, she said to herself, and I will show her what's what.

And then, two days later, a cheque arrived in her name. All the fees for *White Sari* had been made directly to Anju. Now, she read her name, 'Miss Kalai Arasi', written in a big black hand. It was the first payment for the PKB movie. Anju was standing by the bedroom, watching her.

Experimentally, Kalai said, 'From now on, I'd like to open my post myself.'

Anju didn't say anything.

Kalai felt an ugly thrill, a sort of sickening pleasure. 'This is only the beginning, Anju,' she said silently.

Kalai let her strange attraction for PKB grow. She knew

she could stop it any time, clean her mind of his presence and fill it with something else. She knew she had a strong will. When every other girl mooned over a movie hero or a boy from Loyola, Kalai prided herself on her supreme self-control. But now, after the pain of her thwarted romance with the Ooty hero, she allowed PKB to occupy her thoughts, as though he were the antidote to Shekar.

It was a strange feeling. It wasn't as though he was just some handsome man. For one, he was even older than Anju, and she normally didn't pay much attention to people so ancient. And then, she did not even know what he looked like, under the film-star persona and the make-up. And more, she had grown up always knowing him. He was already the number one hero of Tamil cinema before Anju even conceived her. Kalai grew up watching his movies, even reading about him in Anju's Tamil magazines occasionally, so he had been a constant public presence in her life. Now she was making him a private presence. It was like claiming friendship with the statue of Gandhi on the Beach Road. PKB would most likely also have a statue one day on Beach Road. Gandhi, Kannagi, Nehru, Mountbatten, Queen Victoria, PKB.

～

The night after they shot the goodbye song, Anju went to sleep like a lamb. Kalai lay in her best nightgown, restless. She had arrived at the resort with her desire and fear so whipped up that when the bellboy told her PKB's room was right next to hers she knew she had to do something about it. She couldn't let the opportunity slip away, as she had with Shekar. The next morning, they only had a few continuity shots. Then it would indeed be goodbye. They would go back to Madras, to their own homes. She would never be lying so close to PKB, with just a wall between them.

If only she had her own room. She could telephone and invite him for a cup of coffee. But that would be forward as well. How would she put it? Mr PKB, I was wondering if you wanted a cup of coffee? Ha ha ha, Mr PKB, how very amusing. No. She couldn't do it. Her voice would betray her. But she was the excellent actress with natural talent. No, she couldn't do it. But she had to put an end to this agony.

Before she could change her mind, Kalai slipped out of the room, letting the door close behind her. She was outside PKB's door, knocking.

Silence. She held her breath. It was too late. It was done. He would open the door now, and what would she say? There was only silence. He wasn't in his room. He was ... what if someone else was in there? Or ...

The door opened. PKB. No make-up. No wig. Fresh as flowers. He didn't smile. His lips, part of his cheek, twitched. She slipped in before Anju could leap out of her room and seize her.

'Hello, Arasi,' said PKB, shutting the door.

On one side of the bed lay an open book. The reading

lamp glowed yellow. The balcony doors were open to the sea breeze.

~

Kalai had both her hands on PKB's cheeks. She studied his every feature. The skin around his eyes had the finest wrinkles. Those eyes at last exposed to her, unclad.

'You don't need make-up or a wig.' She blew on his hairline, which crowned a high forehead and peaked on either side like a gentle devil's horns.

'Arasi,' said PKB, drawing her to him and laying his cheek against hers. 'You haven't seen me on film without make-up, especially next to heroines half my age. I look terrible.'

'Surely not.'

'I need all the help, believe me.'

She pulled her cheek back and smiled at him. It occurred to her that he was nearly thrice her age, but she didn't say it. Instead, she said, 'I haven't been with anyone before, but I don't feel even a little bit scared.'

'Perhaps you don't. But I am terrified.' He widened his eyes the way he did with Veni in *Azhage Mugam*, then smiled his devastating smile.

'You are beautiful.' She said it simply.

~

The next day they shot the finale of the goodbye song. PKB and Kalai poured emotion. The director declared their joint acting skills had reached a new pinnacle. They gave each other secret smiles. When they mouthed the words for goodbye, Kalai really felt the emotions she was supposed to show. For who knew when she would see him again. She guessed it was going to be the most difficult thing in the world to arrange.

She would worry about it later. Now, they were here, singing together, face-to-face, spilling tears on each other's hands, touching with the tenderness the movie required them to show. They had to caress gently to seduce the movie audience with their grief. They couldn't bite and tear, get into each other with the aid of teeth, hair, blood and skin, so they could not be parted.

No. They sighed gently, came together like feathers, tiptoed away, singing. Kalai felt a comfort in the false reality of the movies. They showed her how to control the uncontrollable.

~

A month later, Kalai received a call. They had decided to include her in the final scene of the movie. Three hours later, she was in costume, on the set, five hundred extras thronging all about.

The insurrection had succeeded. The usurpers had been punished. The prince had returned to his palace, triumphant. He released his mother and father, the queen and king, from their unjust imprisonment. There he stood, in the palace court, surrounded by his lieutenants, friends, well-wishers and his favourite people, the peasants.

'Long live our prince, long live our prince,' went up the cry. The prince bid them calm down. He placed the crown upon his elderly father's head. 'Long live the king,' he started, and they followed faithfully, 'Long live the king.' But the king ordered them to be quiet. The king made a speech. He praised his people for being faithful. He called them his children. The director yelled, 'Cut.' There was a script discussion. *People* in Tamil could also mean children. What other word could be used? PKB said, 'How about *own* children? That clearly differentiates between the two.'

Shooting resumed. The king continued his speech. He praised the lieutenants who had remained true. He praised the soldiers who had remained true. And then finally, he praised his son, the prince, who had proved himself to be a brave, right-minded young man. A worthy successor to the throne, said the king, taking his crown from his head. 'Time to give way to the new generation,' he said. The people surrounding them grinned and swayed with happiness. The prince blushed. The king placed the crown upon his son's head. The son was led to the throne and there he sat and surveyed the court imperiously. 'Long live the king,' went up the cry. 'Long live the king.'

Now his queen made her entrance. Silently, she was led to the king's side. He sat and she stood next to him. They surveyed all.

'Cut,' shouted the director. 'Perfect. Congratulations, everyone. Job well done.'

'Ah,' said Kalai, without meaning to say it aloud.

'Wait,' said PKB. He gazed expectantly at Kalai.

She was forced to share her thoughts. 'The prince should renounce the throne,' she said. 'Declare it a republic. After all, the title of the movie is *People's Champion*.'

'That kind of thing never happened while kings ruled,' said the scriptwriter, not hiding his irritation.

'They never wore these costumes either,' she said. All the male cast were in Robin Hood outfits. Tights, vests, belts and dinky hats. 'It is a fantasy,' she said, 'not a historical documentary.'

'That's true,' said the director.

'It is much more current,' said Kalai. 'Nehru declared India a republic, didn't he? It will be a reference to India's independence from the British. People relish such references.'

Since when had she become an expert on people? Look at me, thought Kalai. Like an election campaigner. PKB had announced recently that he had joined the ruling party. The rose and black should have given her the clue long ago. But the next election was four years away. PKB had the long term in his sights. He was building up a support base to rule forever. She knew he was going to be chief minister one day.

The final scene was reshot. The king placed the crown upon his son's head. The prince removed the crown. Everyone took a step back in astonishment.

PKB announced, 'I did not fight for the freedom of my motherland in order to rule it in a totalitarian way. I have no desire for power. I have no desire to be king.'

The peasants urged him in chorus, 'But you are our only king. You are the ruler of our hearts.'

'I would like to rule your hearts, not your lives,' said PKB. 'I would like to serve my people, not have my people serve me as king.'

'Then who will rule us?' cried the chorus.

'You will rule yourselves,' said PKB. He raised his hand in a fist. 'Long live the people's rule,' he thundered. 'Long live the people's rule.'

The people milled about, delighted.

It was then the queen appeared in a simple sari, shorn of all her queenly attributes.

'What happened to you?' said the astonished prince.

'When you have declared the people's rule here, how can I rule my country as a queen?' said Kalai, head bent sideways in shyness, doodling on the floor with her big toe.

The whole court laughed fondly at what this implied.

She continued, 'I knew this would happen here. That is why . . .'

'That is why?' said PKB.

The lieutenant who used to detest the queen piped in, 'Hear, hear. Our sister-in-law knew our brother's mind before even he did.'

'She did?' said PKB.

'And declared her country a "people's republic" yesterday!'

The court laughed. PKB, still with an astonished face, put his arm around her shoulders and drew her to stand by him.

'My wife is miles ahead of me,' he said. The courtiers collapsed in another bout of mirth. The camera dollyed back to capture the whole court roar with laughter and with joy.

~

People's Champion ran in the cinemas houseful for over a year. Kalai was the number one heroine of Tamil cinema. PKB became more beloved of the Tamil people than Ayya and Gandhi put together.

2005

With one foot curved around a knot joining two ropes, the other on the window ledge of the poor wretch who lived in that part of the building, Mani fished for a box of matches under his filthy lungi. If he had a wife, he thought, he would ask her to wash the lungi. He lit his beedi, dragged on it with pleasure. If he had soap, he thought, he could wash it himself. He looked up and down the unfinished scaffolding, assessed the work to be done. Thanks to the cut-out business, he could afford soap when he finished this job. Perhaps he could afford a wife by the time the CM was re-elected. He looked down at the street, sizing it up as though he were sizing up a prospective wife.

It was a small street. It did not have the typical length and breadth or the volume of traffic preferred by the cut-out aficionados. It was a two-man job, no more. They were erecting the poles slowly, taking their time tying each piece of rope over each joint. After half a day's work, the scaffolding was one-storey high. That was fast enough, decided Mani. It wasn't as if they were paid more if they worked faster.

Mani noted with mild satisfaction the handprint of dust he'd just left on the whitewashed wall beside the window.

The man in the flat to which the window belonged had pulled the shutters close and hung a gunnysack to block himself in, and to block the likes of Mani from getting a look in. No matter, Mani told himself. If there was anything to see in this life, he had seen it already.

The sun burned overhead. It was no time to be high up on the poles. What he needed was a cricket hat. Like that one there. In truth, even with the protection of the hat, the man underneath, new to the job, was struggling. The poles he was tying together collapsed for the second time. Plus, he was no monkey. He needed practice.

'Eda Muthu,' Mani called to the man in the cricket hat.

Muthu, who wore filthy, frayed trousers and a yellow T-shirt that said 'Hello' in English, looked around to see where the voice was coming from. He finally spotted Mani, just a yard above. Muthu's hat was too low on his head. It covered his eyes.

'Want a beedi?' asked Mani.

Muthu shook his head and produced a Goldflake packet from his pocket. Mani climbed down. They both sat on the steps of the building, ignoring the dog within that had been barking all morning and now, sensing them so close, howled with renewed vigour.

'Sssss,' hissed Muthu, fanning himself with his hat. 'What heat, what heat.'

'But good work, no? There are two more to do in the coming week, and who knows, perhaps more?'

'What I don't understand is,' said Muthu, jabbing a

finger in the air like some intellectual, 'why they want to build such an enormous cut-out on this small street.'

Mani surreptitiously looked at the hat which now rested on Muthu's knee as he surveyed the street. It had a label in the front, a logo embroidered on it with the letters 'MCC'. Madras Cricket Club. Mani licked his lips as desire flamed within him.

'The traffic here isn't worth two of Ambur,' said Muthu.

'Rumour is,' said Mani, bending towards Muthu's ear, 'that the MP who is erecting this one has some information that the leaderess will take this road tomorrow as a shortcut.'

'Or for security purpose,' said Muthu, delighted.

'Yes, you catch my point,' added Mani in English, unable to keep his eyes from straying again to the hat.

'Tell me, big brother,' said Muthu. He leaned back against the door and let the Goldflake smoke swirl away from him. 'How long have you lived here, since you left your village?'

The dog started throwing itself against the door in a frenzy of fury. Mani too leaned back, and said, 'Ha, twenty years now, or more. Came with dreams in my eyes . . .'

'To be in the movies.'

'Yes. Not all of us get there, of course. But it has been a good life. I have three autographs from Sathya sir, and one from PKB that I have framed and hung next to the god Murugan. From his very last film, mind.'

Muthu sat up in surprise. 'Did you speak to him? Touch him? Did you act in the film?'

'Oh yes,' said Mani, waving a self-deprecatory hand. 'I was in two crowd scenes. The glory days.'

'The glory days, indeed. No one talks of him nowadays, eh?' Muthu looked like a man with something on his chest. 'There is only one great leader,' he said. He looked around as if fearing to be overheard, although they were alone except for the mad dog. 'It is all about the leaderess now, isn't it?'

'Yes,' said Mani, cautiously.

'She doesn't even mention him in speeches any more.'

'Yes,' said Mani, nodding. It was true.

'Have you noticed the posters?'

'Yes.'

'And the cut-outs?'

'Yes.'

'No more PKB. Just the leaderess, all on her own, and the coconut frond symbol. These big big cut-outs.'

'To be fair,' said Mani, 'it is the ministers that are soaping her by putting up the cut-outs. Look how big their names are in the corner. All so she will know who built it when she passes by.' One thought trailed into another. He would buy soap that evening.

'That may be,' said Muthu, 'but she can see them for what they are, can't she? She is surrounded with jugs and lids that clang at her every utterance.'

'Who can tell what she thinks?'

'With all the noise these jaalras make, she cannot hear the pulse of the common people.'

'Pulse of the common people? You should be writing the Speechwriter's speeches. Show him a thing or two.'

'I could?'

'Well,' said Mani, 'that is enough politics for one day. Come. The boss wants to see the head in place by the end of the day.'

'Say,' said Muthu as they got to their feet. 'What would you ask for one of your autographs?'

'The hat,' said Mani instantly.

'PKB's autograph for this hat?' said Muthu, his eyes enormous pools of joy.

'No, no. I wouldn't exchange my life for PKB's autograph.' Reverence for the great dead man coursed through him.

'Oh.'

'But I will give you one of Sathya's.'

'I'll think about it,' said Muthu. He placed his hat on his head, flicked its brim and pushed the chinstrap in place.

Before climbing back up on the pole, Mani gave the door a good kick. The dog started up again.

~

The Bentley squeezed into the narrow street, and a wave of claustrophobia came over Kalai Arasi. She was never driven through narrow streets any more. Too dangerous. Easy to stop the car. The car had to keep moving. A moving target is difficult to hit. So why now?

With great hesitation, her head of security spoke from the front seat, eyes on the rear-view mirror. 'Madam, the usual route, a bit problematic this morning. Received word just now only. There is some weakness to the Alwarpet bridge.'

'The mini flyover?'

'Yes, madam.'

Built by the last administration. The Speechwriter's son's pet project.

'Is it going to crumble?'

'As I said, madam, it is only some weakness. A crack, I believe. We thought, better not to travel under it.'

Even at fifty miles an hour, they couldn't risk having her spend a half-second speeding under a cracked bridge. Whereas the general public, half a million of them on any given day, rumbled slowly over and under the always congested bridge.

The Bentley had slowed to a crawl. The street had grown even narrower. She could see that an effort had been made to ensure her passage through it was bearable. Debris cleared. Dustbins moved. And they had somehow, improbably, found time to build enormous cut-outs. The lungi-clad backside of a man, missed by her supposedly efficient security, came into view through the Bentley's windscreen. She craned her neck. He was on the scaffolding of an unfinished section of the cut-out, beneath her raised victory sign, finishing the last letter of an MP's name. He who no doubt ordered it built. The man wore a cricket hat. She saw him freeze, paintbrush in hand. Black Cat operatives from either side of the car ran towards him. Ilango stepped on the gas. The Bentley rocketed through the rest of the gap. She hoped they were kind to the man. He was no assassin.

'Put the bridge in the speech,' she said to the man beside her, notepad and pen in hand. Her secretary Vijayan. He began scribbling.

'No, wait, leave it till the crack widens. Let there be some pieces of the bridge falling. Tonight. Let nobody get hurt.'

'Or perhaps, madam, just a small head injury?'

Kalai thought better than to respond to that.

She said, 'We will make a statement tomorrow.'

'Yes, madam. Also, that way we will get two headlines, one for today's announcement, and one for tomorrow's condemnation.'

'Today's announcement. I'm not so sure.'

'Madam?'

'It will seem like we are desperate. Still using PKB to get the people's vote.'

'But it is a positive association, madam. People love PKB films still.'

Kalai looked away from him, irritated. He was right, her secretary. Used to be PKB's secretary. She saw no reason yet to replace him.

~

Along with the cut-outs, flags and bunting, a plastic Christmas tree adorned the entrance of KA TV. One bunting, about three men wide and five long, proclaimed in black and rose lettering over white: '10TH ANNIVERSARI KA TV'.

Stepping into the fanfare from her Bentley, Kalai wondered if she was the only one there who noticed the spelling error. So many journalists. Pens and pads, dictaphones. Television crews with cameras and bright lights, lens-nosed photographers. All in such a hurry to get ahead with their careers, they didn't stop to learn their spellings. Of course, she was simply finding reasons to put down journalists. Journalists were the new enemy. What did she do to deserve their ire? If she did any good for the people, they called it a populist move. If she did something unpopular, they called her arrogant.

What did journalists have to do with the bunting, she thought, as she smiled and pressed her palms in greeting, raising them slightly towards the persons she recognised. Those present were from her own papers, her dailies, weeklies, monthlies, and the TV channel. And some neutral ones, if one could use the word 'neutral' at all for journalists. Like that greybeard from *The Hindu*. A rich intellectual. Whereas the poor man whose job it was to make these signs, to paint them, what did he know what an 'anniversary' was, in that foreign tongue which was used constantly – even sixty years after the foreigners themselves left – to put the poor man in his place?

She moved slowly through the crowd, the TV staff, people from the party, the diehards. Her presence infused reverence, stillness, a sticky molasses quality in the crowd that made it impossible for her to move briskly through it. With her palms still pressed together, she entered the building. Inside, there were still more people to press palms to, and then, even slower, she progressed into the auditorium, where she would make the announcement. More than half her days were spent pressing and raising her palms. Her forearms ached. Everyone knew, of course, that her nod was as sincere as pressed palms. Still.

Bodies squeezed, a commingling of perfumes and sweat, to make way for her, up the two steps to the stage. Thankfully, she was yet to have any trouble from the press when, on occasion, her arms became too painful to lift. At least she did not have to shake hands with every one of them. She reached her seat. Some sheets of paper on the table. Her speech. The edges of the papers like gradations in a palm-fan. She pushed them neatly together. Even the Swiss and the Swede came to meet her thoroughly briefed on the Indian female's etiquette, and didn't do anything silly like grabbing her hand for a shake. A short microphone stooped over a vase of flowers on the tablecloth. It hummed like a bee. She swept her eyes over the backdrop. Her pixellated image filled it, pressing palms demurely, eyes lowered just a bit, but, somehow, improbably, looking straight and clear into the public's eye. All on her own, with the coconut frond. No Ayya, no PKB hovering in miniature over her shoulder to give her their blessing. There she was, with her symbols and colours, alone.

She sat down.

Even as the tea leaves stained the boiling water, rage stained MLA Poongothai's being. She was reading the latest slur on the chief minister as she made the tea. How dare they treat the CM as though she were some two-bit politician who could be held accountable to the clamouring of mad dogs? Poongi fumed. She was the mother, wasn't she? If PKB was the Tamil people's father, the CM was their mother. Holy mother.

Still reading, she switched off the stove and poured the tea. She gave one tumbler to her husband, and set the other on the dining table. She sat down to continue reading. She paused a moment to think, I am Poongothai, Member of the Legislative Assembly. So she felt not only rage, but also the righteousness of her rage. She came to the end of the article. She trembled.

'Why are you torturing yourself by reading such nonsense?' said her husband.

She did not answer.

'Let me tear it up,' he said and snatched the newspaper from her.

She snatched it back. 'The election is coming,' she said.

She would read the article again, quote from it later, as necessary. At public meetings, for instance, to stoke the voting crowd's ire. She finished her tea, and her stomach was in no state for breakfast. Next to her was a pile of the Tamil dailies, which she had already read through. Sweeping *The Hindu* towards the pile, she raised her hands to knot her damp hair into a bun. She realised what she had to do.

Waiting outside the door were that day's people come to see her. Good people, with the money or without the money, all wanting something. All wanting Poongothai MLA's guidance.

'Tell them all to come tomorrow,' she told her husband.

Then she went into the small backyard and began collecting leaves. Election was coming. Mylapore, the seat she wanted. Porur, the seat she was given. One accepted what one was given. But Mylapore, with its superior brahmins and famous temples, was the constituency she was meant to serve. Porur was the backwater where she had relatives. The gods lived in the Mylapore temples.

Rhythmically, almost hypnotically, her hands reached and plucked, reached and plucked the mango leaves, and dropped them into the plastic bucket. How dare they! On the surface it was a small write-up about the CM attending the tenth anniversary celebrations of KA TV, her brainchild, and announcing bonuses to all the employees in celebration of the occasion. But did the CM stop with that? No. The big announcement. The great gift to the masses: one PKB movie a day, to be aired at 1 p.m. till eternity. The dear leaderess had declared, 'The eternal light of our dear departed permanent leader of the party' – how she never stopped telling everyone she was merely the secretary of the party – 'will be tended and kept alive by this simple measure, by the light of the TV station, which glows and acts as a beacon, a torch, in honour of his twin greatnesses, as entertainer without peer and as a peerless leader of the people.'

Journalists, they must all be sent to the villages to work the land, till the soil, sow and harvest paddy, break their backs. Only then could they claim to be the real voice of the people. A bunch of overeducated eunuchs with connections. Daddy got him the job. Now he thinks he can write. Poongothai's hand trembled, and the leaf she held between thumb and forefinger trembled too. She let it fall into the bucket, and it did so in a twirl, slowed by its own grace and the buffeting air. Divine grace.

Diminishing popularity, indeed. Desperate attempt to win back the *peasant* population, indeed. Cheap, garish gimmick, said the article. As if the other party did anything that wasn't cheap or gimmicky. There was something or the other every day in the papers to tarnish the leaderess. She was looking fey lately. Poongothai paused a moment, then brought the leaf she'd just plucked to her nose. This, *this*, will set her right, will restore her waning powers, her health and influence. She dropped the leaf into the bucket.

~

She spent the rest of the morning sewing in the back of the kitchen. The activity required purity and penance. Thankfully, it was not her time of the month, or she would have lost several days of good rage. She sat on the hard floor. No relief through a mat or a chair. To do it comfortably rubbed against the grain of the whole idea. Who was that woman in a fairy tale, who sewed and sewed for release from a curse? She did it on the floor. A Russian fairy tale?

Early eighties. Lots of Russian culture. The good days. Now all American. Soon, African. The world turned and changed.

Poongothai was solid as a stone. Village heart, city brain. All this English Shminglish. The CM, so modest. Her English would make an Englishman open his jaws wide in astonishment. But she never spoke it unless absolutely necessary. Only with foreign dignitaries and with the northern leaders. The CM could speak Hindi of course, like a duck could speak water. But Hindi was an enemy tongue, pure Dravidian that she was. And these silly journalists, going to schools like DAV and Shishya, 'What ya, this ya, that ya,' showing off in English. You couldn't even go to the grocery store without some fair-skinned bimbo in a cotton sleeveless top pointing at a pile of curry leaves and asking 'How much this is?' as if speaking in Tamil would degrade her to the status of *peasants*.

She pricked her thumb. Direct the rage, the goddess was saying to her. She sucked on the tip till the bleeding stopped. She applied her mind to the style and length of the costume. Applied her mind to its engineering requirements, because it was imperative, simply imperative, that the whole structure stay up.

Soon, through the husband, through the servant, word spread. When she was ready, there were three women waiting to help her. People thronged the front of the house to get behind her on the journey.

But when she came out of the house, the rage evaporated. She felt naked, for all the foliage covering her. It wasn't proper clothing. So flimsy, held up by her own sewing. With all the eyes fixed upon her, she felt stripped like a tree of its bark. Raw, naked, fragile. A snail. A kid. No more a raging inferno speeding towards the goddess. She felt the string on her waist slip, and she clasped it with a hiss of escaping breath. The husband twittered nervously. It was better he stayed out of her sight. She paused at the gates of her house, the people gathering behind her.

She could not face the long walk to the temple of the Devi. So she hailed an auto. One of the women got in beside her. The auto driver only gave her a cursory glance. Didn't even blink.

'To the temple,' she said, using her parliamentary voice.

He nodded from side to side like a marionette. What were all of them but puppets in the hands of the goddess? She was doing as the Devi commanded. She was a mere mortal, without a will of her own. All the will and purpose and action was the Devi's, the mother's. The Devi held fast the loose leaves strung around her waist in rows upon rows. The Devi held fast the loose leaves strung around her breasts in rows upon rows. The Devi guided her hands as they sewed the mango leaves one by one. The Devi guided her eyes towards the mango tree, rather than the neem tree only a yard away. Neem leaves, the Devi knew, did not hold as fast as mango leaves. They were smaller, so more difficult to sew together, harder to keep in place. The Devi even now kept Poongothai's mind off the discomfort of the mango leaf stalks sticking and digging into her skin upon the thin, worn auto seat.

They turned into the road. The temple of the Devi stood at the end. Poongothai stoked the rage back into the heart that had mellowed with those pure thoughts about the Devi. She would show those that dared question the will of the Devi. She would cast the first stone that would then lead to many other stones being cast. A return to the old ways, to faith, to bhakti, which need not be incompatible with progress and education. After all, she had a BA from Madras University, didn't she? In folk music. And the music sprang from peasants who toiled in the midday heat and then sang praises to the Devi who gave them good harvests. It was important to remember these things in the face of the relentless march of obscenity cloaked in the guise of modernity. All these western thoughts and habits, propagated by these DAV-educated city journalists who did nothing but sneer at old ways, the simple ways, sneer at tradition and the CM who was so good, so good, she had personally encouraged Poongi to become something in politics, to do something that changed things. Well, now she would change things.

'Can you hear me?' the auto driver was saying. 'I said, fifty rupees on the meter.' He tapped the meter.

Cars and autos screeched to a halt around them. Her husband, the other women and followers bounded out. They stood waiting.

The auto driver said, 'OK, give what you want. Even ten rupees is fine. For an auspicious undertaking such as this.'

Poongothai ignored the auto driver. She was gathering herself.

'OK, let it be free. Put in a good word for me with the goddess.' He nodded his head from side to side. Puppet.

The sharp stalks of the mango leaves underneath her. The sticky sliding on the seat as the auto jostled. The Devi demanded that her actions were to be absolutely pure. Wearing underwear would be to cheat. A tree beside the temple swayed its branches in the sudden breeze, as if beckoning her. The Devi was beckoning her. Put your faith in the Devi. She would make sure not a single mango leaf came loose. The Devi will protect your chastity, one hundred per cent.

She stepped out of the auto, swaying gently, rocking from side to side. The Devi was coming upon her. The devotees cheered. Women began ululating. Men clapped their hands against their cheeks. Some swayed as she did. People gathered.

'We will go to the Devi in the temple for her blessings for our leaderess, the CM,' said Poongothai, in a high, wavery, intoxicated voice. 'Then we will walk all the way to her house and offer her the Devi's prasadam and blessings.'

As she rocked her way into the temple, to a trumpeting of ululations from the women and Devi-praise from the men, Poongothai spoke to the Devi within her. 'I put my trust in you, Devi. You will not let loose a single leaf from my garment.'

The image of a lone leaf came to her mind, lolling partly underneath the metal rim of the auto, inches from her foot as she had made to step out. She pushed that image away. It wasn't from her costume. It was some other leaf.

It looked like a pirangi leaf. She had one hundred per cent trust in the Devi.

To great fanfare, she entered the temple. The priests, those Mylapore brahmins, came crashing out of the altars. They slapped their cheeks to purify themselves for her gaze. She spied a stone pillar with an enclave full of vermilion. She grabbed some and threw it around. Anoint the faithful. Someone started a chant. Poongi began a dance, uncaring of the mango leaves. The dance would obliterate her enemies. The CM was going to be impressed. The CM would be moved, and she would bless them all.

~

When Kalai Arasi came down the sweeping staircase of her mansion, she was greeted by the sickly smell of lily and jasmine. A man-tall garland with the two flowers intertwined, wrapped in clear polythene, lay on the sofa.

Before she could step off the staircase, Vijayan thrust the diary under her nose.

'Schedule, madam,' he said.

She pushed it away and said, 'Why is it so white? Where is the usual rose and marigold?'

She saw the confusion in all the faces in the receiving hall. Each face gazed in ignorance at another for an answer, for support.

Ilango finally met her eyes and said, 'I bought it, madam, for a change.'

'Why?'

'I thought it would stand apart from the Speechwriter's garland. Last year, I noticed the garlands were exactly the same.'

In fact, thought Kalai, the last ten years, the garlands had been exactly the same. It would be no surprise to her if the same nursery supplied the garlands, the same woman made them.

Even through the cellophane, the smells of jasmine and lily were intense. She felt the tentacle of a headache curl around the front of her head.

'No,' she said. 'It isn't auspicious to change the way we do things so close to the elections. Get the rose garland.'

'The garland is for Ayya,' said Ilango. 'He started the Progress for Dravidians Party.'

'So?' What was Ilango's point?

'He started it as a movement against superstition, supporting rationalism, did he not? And we are going to garland him.'

'Are you calling me superstitious?' she said. One or two men in the hall held their breath, eyes swivelling from her to Ilango, fearfully waiting for a blowout. Really, when had she ever lost her temper?

Ilango did not answer. He had little frown lines on his forehead. He must have set his heart on the white garland.

'Why white, Ilango?'

'It is the colour of goddess Saraswati. I thought Ayya would approve.'

Kalai laughed. So much for *her* superstition. Didn't

Ayya denounce the gods as the weapons of the oppressors?

'Ayya was an atheist,' said Kalai. 'We are all atheists, we politicians. We who wield power. Secular, rational and atheist. Remember?'

Ilango looked a little perplexed. 'Well, Saraswati, learning, it is only a symbol,' he stammered.

It seemed to matter to him, thought Kalai, that she pick this stinking white garland for Ayya. Could she do this for Ilango? Give in to him in front of all these men, minions, watching hungrily?

'Get me the rose garland.'

Before Ilango could reply, Vijayan came and buzzed.

'What is it?' she said.

'The Speechwriter,' said Vijayan, twitching nervously, 'he has it seems decided to garland Ayya before us.'

'Now?'

'He's starting now, from R. Nagar.'

Fury. She garlanded Ayya every year on his birth anniversary. Ten in the morning. The first among all the political leaders. The Speechwriter, by unspoken agreement, always went in the afternoon. Until now. The guts of the man, to try to supersede her.

'Let us go now,' she said to Vijayan. 'Tell the traffic police to hold him up.'

They began to move towards the door. Casually, she flung at Ilango, 'The white one will do.' He nodded, looking relieved. Casting an eye towards the watching men, she snapped, 'But only this once.' Then she swept out, with her entourage.

However, she had barely put a foot into the car when she noticed a commotion at the gates.

Of all the sights that should meet her eyes. Poongothai MLA came dancing into her compound clad only in a dress of leaves. Her head reeled. How should she react to *this*?

Kalai too, a long time ago, had grabbed the headlines, worn a dress made of flowers for a movie. A PKB film, of course. But there had been flesh-coloured panelling underneath. Poongothai, with all her bits jiggling, Kalai felt certain, was nude under the leaves.

'My queen,' squawked the woman, eyes wide and bloodshot, hair mussed and tangled from the dance. There were at least a dozen men and women with her, reverent and frightened at the same time – of the goddess descended on Poongi, or of herself, Kalai could not tell.

Impatiently she mouthed the right words, took the blessing, blessed in return, looked at the imaginary watch on her wrist, cleared her throat once or twice, before she could be on her way.

When the cavalcade was turning on to Cathedral Road, she said, 'Wait, let us U-turn, go via Royapettai High Road.' She knew they would hold the Speechwriter as long as was necessary for her to get to the statue.

'Yes, madam,' said Ilango, even though nobody else was in the car. He did not ask why. He knew it was to pick up Selvi.

They turned on to a leafy road behind Royapettai High Road and collected Selvi, all primped and waiting by the door.

When Selvi was in the car, both Ilango and Kalai had a friend. The garland lay across the front passenger seat. Selvi sat beside Kalai.

'Selvi,' said Kalai, 'look at that garland Ilango decided to get for Ayya.'

'All white is unusual, isn't it?' said Selvi.

'Unusual is a diplomatic way of putting it,' said Kalai.

Selvi said, 'Appearances matter. Colour matters. If you wear gold, you are a wealthy woman. White may be a fashionable colour in some parts of the world, but here it merely indicates an absence of colour. It is devoid of the auspiciousness that red and yellow possess.'

'But it is superstitious to assign auspiciousness to colours,' whined Ilango from the front.

'Enough of that, Ilango.'

Irritation pricked Kalai. It was the tone of his voice. Of course Ilango was a friend to her, just as Selvi was. In fact, Ilango was her oldest friend. Today, though, he was like an uppity servant. It was his own fault, of course. He did not know how to behave with her. Slavish sometimes, avuncular otherwise. During her years of political infancy, he had even advised her, seen her cry, fantastical though that memory now seemed.

'Selvi, how are the wedding preparations coming along?'

'All good. Got the hall we wanted, priests we asked for, procured even the caterers who are impossible to get.'

'I would like to meet someone who would say no to us.'

'Indeed,' Selvi laughed. 'The bride, of course, said no at first.'

'Yes, she thought Dayalan was chubby from the photo, did she not? Remind me, what made her change her mind?'

Kalai liked to hear this story. It appealed to her younger self, the romantic in her.

'Chubby went on diet, sent her another photo one month later.'

Kalai smiled. 'We must stop calling him Chubby.'

She had a sudden inspiration. 'Let's prepone the wedding.'

'What?' said Ilango and Selvi, almost together.

'Yes,' she said. 'Charming young couple. Everyone loves a wedding. It's auspicious.'

Ilango, still with that irritating, subversive voice, said, 'Weddings are miserable affairs in our part of the world. It is only at funerals that people come together, smile, laugh, dance.'

'You weren't at my wedding,' said Kalai. 'It was a very happy occasion.' She, too, had married for love, for tenderness, once. All that the marriage had softened in her, she saw now, became hardened by politics, the way manual labour causes palms to callus.

'I will always regret missing your wedding, baby,' said Ilango, suddenly the old Ilango. She felt a little of her ill will towards him subsiding. It came to her with startling clarity: a vision of the end of her days. Ilango and she doddering together, bickering. It made her smile.

'We will have a grand celebration,' she said to Selvi. 'Free for all. Feed everyone. Do not even think about the expenditure. No limit on the budget. The wedding will wash away this bad, this . . .' – she waved her arm – 'cloying feeling among the people, this fear. Let us have a grand procession. Next month.'

'Next month?' said Selvi. 'I just had everyone agree to the 18th of July.'

'No. Let it be the first week of May.'

'But that is two weeks before the election,' said Ilango.

'Yes, that is the whole point,' said Kalai. 'It is auspicious to have a wedding for my adopted son before the elections.'

'Adopted in name only,' growled Ilango in an undertone.

'Shut up, Ilango,' said Kalai, but took the edge off her voice with a smile. 'And no white garlands at the wedding, mind.'

Selvi laughed, delighted. 'Splendid idea,' she said. 'Let me off here. I have to go make all the arrangements, again.'

'No chance,' said Kalai. 'I need you beside me to tackle the Speechwriter.'

~

The Marina beach statue of Ayya, black granite usually bird-splattered a motley grey, gleamed for her visit. Whoever had taken the trouble to clean it that morning had not, she noticed, been able to get the birdshit out of the statue's hair. Ayya had salt-and-pepper hair as a result, just as he did in real life, as seen by Kalai in various newsreels, for she had never met him in person. The rest of him was jet black, as if parodying the dark Dravidians whom he had championed all his life.

Another parody of the Dravidian – short, squat and very dark – was the Speechwriter. She first saw the gleam of his trademark fluorescent green shawl, then the man himself appeared out of his Tata Sumo. He had to hop down from the car to the ground. A small man from a big car. She was pleased to have garlanded Ayya, said her piece to the cameras assembled, posed humbly for the obligatory photos, all before the Speechwriter arrived. He looked extremely annoyed at being beaten to the front of the queue.

In spite of resolving, at Selvi's insistence, to play it cool, she said, sweet as saccharine, 'Late as usual, Mr Velu?'

A brilliant smile split the wizened old face. She prepared herself for his oratorical genius.

'Better late than never, Miss Arasi.'

She was disappointed. She had not expected such a cliché.

The cameras swooped upon them, journalists muttering to each other and shouting to them to shake hands, pose together. No one was interested in hearing what they actually said to each other.

What should she say to him? He was waiting, confident of some kind of triumph. He had the same lilt to his voice as PKB did. PKB also liked to call her Miss Arasi. These men, she thought. They owned everything they surveyed. The arrogance of the man shone even in the way he said Miss Arasi.

'Let us shake hands, Mr Velu,' she said.

He frowned. The cameras were running, photographers

flashed, clicked. Hesitantly, he put out a hand. She put her palms together. She saw in his eyes the realisation of what she was doing.

'Cheap trick, Miss Arasi,' he said.

'All is fair in politics and war, Mr Velu,' she said, with a smile as if she was enquiring after the family.

The Speechwriter's eyes gleamed hard as oiled nails. He returned the smile. 'Of course, Miss Arasi, but turning tricks suits not a political profession, but another kind.'

Her smile faltered. How could she combat such vileness? Without a further word, she walked away.

She got in the car and said to Selvi, 'Headlines in our papers tomorrow: Speechwriter's Impropriety Mars Ayya's Anniversary Display.'

'Oh?' said Selvi.

'Or better, CM Upholds Womanly Virtue by Refusing to Shake Hands with Speechwriter.'

'Bit long for a headline,' Ilango sniped, but she didn't care.

The accompanying photo would be of Kalai looking demure, pressing palms, and the Speechwriter, his hand mid-air, with an anticlimactic expression on his face.

'A cheap shot,' she admitted to Selvi.

'But worth it,' said Selvi, who did not have a noble vein in her.

'Use what you have,' said Ilango, sighing.

She ignored Ilango. She had to remember what the Speechwriter said to her about turning tricks. A flush spread from her neck to her cheeks. Selvi was talking, not noticing her distraction, her discomfiture. Kalai would remember the insult. She would find a way to make him pay for it.

1975

Clamour assailed Kalai's sleep. She woke wincing and peering at the daylight. The noise was not from her dreams. It came from just outside her closed door. Preparations were under way. She raised herself up. She ought to have leapt out of bed, full of anticipation, excitement. Her spirits, she supposed, would improve when she saw Shekar. She stood, adjusted her nightie, sat in front of the vanity. Took a brush to her hair.

Her image from the poster of *People's Champion* on the opposite wall seemed from some dream puppet world. Ten years had changed her appearance. She was plumper. Her breasts had become something to reckon with. Her face had lost its innocence. More hair crowded her temples. Anju maintained that waxing would roughen her facial skin and make her grow a beard. Kalai pulled in her lips, inspected her chin.

The door opened and the maid, Pushpa, came in.

'Scowling bride,' she said, shaking her head and grinning. She set a tumbler of coffee down. Then she circled her hands above Kalai's head and bent her knuckles to her own temples, removing the glance of the 'evil eyes' from Kalai's countenance.

'That's enough,' said Kalai. 'You go now.'

'Drink quickly and come and eat tiffin,' said Pushpa. Still grinning, she let herself out. For once, she remembered to shut the door behind her.

Kalai sipped her coffee, wishing to be alone a little longer. Once married, she wouldn't be able to dawdle uninterrupted. By children, husband, in-laws, servants. But she was hungry. So she got up, tumbler in hand, and opened the door.

In the hall outside sat women making chains of flowers – jasmine and marigold, baskets of them. One or two were relatives she recognised. A woman she did not know said to her, 'Is this the time to get up? Go, go, have your tiffin.'

They looked as if they had never missed a day's tiffin in their lives, tyre-tubes of fat at their waistbands. In the dining room too, women sat on the floor or at the table chopping vegetables. They were preparing lunch, here at the house, for the hundred or so core group of relatives and help, before they left for the marriage hall.

The evening meal, for seven hundred people, would be eaten on the dining level at the marriage hall. The wedding breakfast tomorrow was for a thousand people, then lunch for five hundred, including reporters. Fans – about two thousand were expected – could come and get a souvenir photo of her and Shekar, along with the usual coconut, laddoo and a banana in a small drawstring bag. She had suggested they print 'Kalai weds Shekar' on the bags. Anju thought it was too radical; nobody she knew had printed souvenir bags. Kalai overruled Anju. It had been her only victory. In every other matter of the wedding preparations, Anju had laid down the law.

Kalai waited, seated at the end of the dining table where they had cleared some space for her. Vegetables and aunts had moved, but the tiffin made no appearance. Pushpa dashed out from the kitchen. 'Two minutes,' she said. 'I am steaming fresh idlis special for you, baby.'

Fresh idlis special for her meant she would have to suffer hunger a bit longer.

'I will come back,' said Kalai, and got up. She left the room to look for Anju. In the next room, women were preparing big round trays of trousseau. Coconuts, sweets, money, jewellery, silk saris. Some women, too old or too young to be useful, or just no good at tasks, sat gossiping on woven mats, sipping coffee, folding handkerchiefs into their blouses. The sweat and talcum powder, the crushed jasmine flowers and the mothballed silk saris made her head swim.

'Come and sit down with us,' said one woman.

But if she did, how could they then gossip about the bride? She wondered how many times PKB had been mentioned.

Another exhorted her to shower and change into a silk sari. Kalai smiled at them all rather than scowling. Her head thumping with hunger now, she went to the front of the house.

A bullock cart was wedged between the gates of the house. The bullocks stamped and dropped dung. From the back of the cart, men unloaded stacks of metal chairs. A shamiana was half erected over the quarter-furlong space outside the front door and reached just over the cut banana trees tied to the gateposts. This would provide shade for the male guests who were already cracking open the newly unloaded chairs and settling themselves into them, chewing betel in their white best. The women would run around, organising and instructing the priests, the flowermen, the sweetmen, the coffee–tea men, the drivers, the cooks, the sweepers. The men would do nothing but sit and be plied with food and drink for the next two days.

Anju was arguing with the bullock cart driver. He looked beaten. Anju shushed him when he made some feeble protest. She thrust notes into his hands. If Ilango had been there, Anju would not have been cutting bargains with cart drivers. There was her brother, Ganesh, still and cool and quiet, become quite inaccessible, talking to his brother-in-law by the drumstick tree. He had no interest in helping with the wedding. A long drumstick bent down from a branch, touching the top of his head. Kalai smiled at him, feeling a little formal. He was slender as a drumstick himself. He caught her eye, smiled back, but there was no warmth there to truly bridge the distance.

'Go in, go in, why are you standing here?' Anju was beside her, gesturing with her hands, shooing her like a dog.

A bullock farted as the cart moved off. All the workmen had stopped and were staring at her. Without Ilango beside her, Kalai felt all too naked in the eyes of men. She drew back and went into the kitchen for her tiffin.

~

Kalai ate breakfast, subjected herself to four women who dressed and decorated her, and climbed into the car that would take her to the wedding hall. In her 'arriving' sari and pearl set, Kalai took up half the back seat of the big Ambassador. Beside her, Anju wore her own wedding sari. Ganesh sat in the front passenger seat. Kalai did not know if the shirt and trousers on him were new or not. Men outside the movie industry did not care about what they wore.

A blast of horn.

'Good, good,' said Anju. 'Keep pressing the horn till we reach the wedding hall. It will attract auspiciousness.'

Kalai rolled her eyes. Accumulation of good fortune had made Anju develop all kinds of superstitions. The driver, what was his name, honked again. He was not Ilango. Weighed down by her sari and jewels, Kalai was also weighed down by Ilango's absence.

～

She had found him sitting at the door of their house with his bundle of clothes and bedding, one morning shortly after *People's Champion* was released.

'I will work for you, baby,' he said to her, a guileless smile on his face. 'You need someone.'

Kalai was overwhelmed that a grown man should offer to dedicate his life to running her errands. She looked to Anju, who said, 'Yes, we do need someone permanent. But I was going to get a girl. We cannot have a man in a house of women.'

Kalai found herself saying, 'But a man is exactly what we need in a house of women.'

That was not the only reason. She liked Ilango. All that time he had acted as her gofer on the set of *People's Champion*, she had never once felt self-conscious in his presence. Other men made her nervous. It was not so much in what they said or did, as the very way in which they occupied space. They seemed to somehow spill over their own allotted space and encroach upon hers, steal a little of her air even, to leave her constantly constricted and short of breath. Ilango was the only man who didn't make her feel that way. And even Anju, she knew, found him a calming presence.

So Ilango moved into their flat. He slept in the front room and ate with them. When Anju decided they needed a bigger house, he found it for them. He dealt with the broker and all the repairs. When the time came, he gave his opinion on the choice of a manager and secretary. He became close friends with PKB's own right-hand man, Murali, although when Kalai and PKB had a disagreement, he fiercely took her side, as Murali did PKB's. And when, like all film stars overindulged by the public and fans and media, Kalai, despite her good sense, started having mood swings and throwing tantrums, it was he, not Anju, who bore the brunt of them.

She would fling a costume and say, 'I won't wear it; it's too dowdy.'

He would laugh and say, 'You are playing a happily married mother of three, so can't go hoofing about in skirts.'

She would sulk about some perceived insult. Find ways to insult him. She would call him a bumpkin, an illiterate. Several times she called him an idiot. He never took it personally. She always apologised. He liked to say, 'You are apologising like you killed my mother.'

~

'Stop grinning,' said Anju in the car. 'Practise your bride face.'

Kalai stopped grinning and practised a demure expression. It was ridiculous that she had to 'act' as the bride at her own wedding. She tried to think of sad things to keep the wistful expression on her face. Ilango would laugh.

Ilango it was who had told her it was time to retreat from the glare of PKB. Like the sun, PKB had been scorching her for ten years. It was time to shelter, to rest, be restored by night, by moonlight. Shekar was her moon.

A smile crept up Kalai's face again. Paradoxically, tears stung her eyes. As the promise of Pushpa's idlis invoked a long, hunger-filled wait, her wedding to Shekar invoked the painful purging of PKB from her life.

After ten years of PKB in their lives, day in and day out, the claustrophobia he brought with him, his overpowering personality, his quick mind and tongue that left everyone a step behind, panting, the cloying politicians who hovered around him, the hundreds of people who materialised wherever he went, hysterically trying to touch him or speak to him, his absence had blown the roof off their lives. Air and light came flooding in. Everything about Shekar was free and easy and delightful. And yet . . .

The wedding hall came in sight. The car stopped at the entrance.

'Wait here,' said Anju. 'I'll go and check if our room is ready first.'

She got out of the car with difficulty in her heavy sari and went in. Kalai too, got out of the car.

Ganesh was out and gone from view.

'Park close by,' she said to the driver.

'I'll park right over there, madam,' he said.

She waited for Anju outside the entrance. Marigolds covered the stucco facade of the building. Giant oil lamps were already lit. An unmanned reception desk waited with its trays of candied sugar, red rose petals and rose water. The musicians were nearby, cleaning their instruments. One among them, sandalwood coating his bald head, put a trumpet to his mouth and blew a short blast.

Anju came out with a coconut. She flung it on the doorstep. It broke, sounding like a cinematic gunshot. Brown shell and white flesh scattered. In an instant a group of children had swooped in from the street. They gathered the coconut pieces. Kalai went into the hall.

~

That evening, Kalai, wearing her 'groom's welcome' sari and her ruby set, surrounded by the women of her extended family, sat on stage and watched the doorway of the marriage hall erupt with the pee-pee dum-dum arrival of the groom's party.

Over the rows of chairs half filled with guests, she saw Anju rush with a plate of vermilion water, a camphor flame in the middle, to welcome her son-in-law.

Her groom. He grinned like a foreigner as Anju inexpertly swung the aarti plate in front of his face. Kalai had the urge to run up and hold her hands in front of Shekar's face, to protect him from the camphor flame.

And here he was, coming to sit beside her on stage so they could welcome the guests together. He wore white bell bottoms, still the Kannada hero, and a brilliant blue shirt with big, pointy collars and long sleeves. His hair curled and domed upon his head. His sideburns and moustache were trimmed and waxed. Even when he didn't catch her eye, focused as he was on grappling with garlands and aunts, having to turn the correct way, sit in a particular fashion, she knew he was desiring and loving and worshipping her.

When he finally caught her eye, Kalai, her own blouse with puffed short sleeves and a high back, more sixties than seventies, hair pressed flat and braided like a peasant girl's, couldn't help but smile at him. An aunt immediately hissed, 'Pull your teeth in and look demure.'

So she did, cowed momentarily, even though she was a superstar worth lakhs of rupees and wizened old directors spoke to her with their mouths covered. Some aunts could cow even the Himalayas.

～

That night, in the bride's room adjoining the stage, Kalai removed all her jewellery. Day one was over. Bride and groom would rest one last night in separate rooms. Anju sat beside her, putting the jewels away. Anju's upper arms wobbled as she snapped shut the velvet boxes. Increasing prosperity had led to a physical flourishing. Her cheeks, chubby and rose coloured, gave her the look of being determinedly happy, which she was. She sighed as the lid closed on the last piece of gold, and sighed again as Kalai embarked on the long process of removing all the hairpins on her head.

'If only Ilango was here,' said Anju, 'he would have taken over all this organising from me. I could have stood at the doors all prettied up, welcoming guests with a sprinkle of rose water, instead of whirling like a dervish between the kitchen and the side entrance.'

'He could have come to the wedding at least,' said Kalai. 'I'll never forgive him.'

Here she was, at the cusp of such a momentous change in her life, and none of the important people were present, excepting Anju and Ganesh, who were family in any case.

Also absent was PKB, who had been her sun. Kalai pulled a hairpin too quickly and out came a few strands of hair. Her eyes watered. Ten years' relationship. Day in and day out. But now, as absent as he had been those three days when he lay unconscious in the ICU of Apollo Hospital. His hand on the cover, faintly twitching, tubes running from it. She had kept a fearful eye on the tick-ticking monitors. She had stared so hard at him his skin looked more translucent by the second. She had held his feet, rough soles, soft ankles, as if pulling him back. They had to push her away forcibly in order to treat him. And then she had camped outside the door. She would neither eat nor drink till he was declared out of danger.

Then his wife arrived, who had been delayed on her way from ... Hyderabad? Delhi? Like a deer in headlights. But then her expression changed. Hard. Kalai was led out. Someone gripped her hand. The wife had tears in her eyes as she faced the mass of tubes and equipment that seiged her unconscious husband. The door shut. Kalai hadn't a single tear. Countenance like stone. It saved her from the gossip rags. People milling the hospital, reporters among them. They had assumed she was being treated too, as she had been present at the incident. They hadn't all the details, not then.

She fled from the hospital after his wife arrived, holed up in her room, in a half light, half gloom of misery and heat. It was the height of summer and she couldn't bear the AC. She had lain in a fever of dreaming for days. Had only become properly self-aware again when the phone rang and she heard a croak from his battered throat down the line.

That was what PKB had meant to her. She pulled free the last of the hairpins.

Anju sighed again. She said, as if she had read her thoughts all along, 'I wish you'd invited PKB. People will talk.'

She had thought about it. Deliberated over it. In the end she had decided to post an invitation. She had spent nearly an hour unable to bring herself to address the envelope, before realising she did not have his address.

'I didn't have his address, Anju.'

Anju guffawed. 'Anyone could have given you his address.'

She had never needed to know his address before. What am I to him, she had thought, that I do not even know his address? Never been to his home? She could not claim friendship with him. She had not a right over him as Anju did over her or his wife did over him. Yet how could she pretend he was merely a senior colleague or a mentor? She did not put him on a pedestal, like the entire state. She had held him close to her heart. Yes, like a friend, but more than that.

Kalai turned away from her face in the mirror, which shone bare like the moon without make-up and flowers and hairpins.

Anju lay down, hummed a song.

She stopped humming to say, 'Have you invited any of your friends from school? They would have liked to come.'

'I did not have their addresses either.'

'Brush your hair,' said Anju. 'There won't be any time to wash it in the morning.'

Kalai loosened her hair and took a brush to it. Bits of dried jasmine fell from the strands, and a missed, twisted hairpin.

'Pinky was my only real friend,' she said to Anju. 'But …' She shrugged, not wanting to say too much.

She had no friends now. Pinky had given her address

in Manali, but Kalai didn't invite her. Her erstwhile best friend.

She had only spoken once to Pinky in the past ten years. It was an accidental meeting. She had been dining in a five-star hotel in Manali. They were shooting a song there. She saw Pinky by a pot plant, across the restaurant. Fat, refined and subdued in a tasteful sari, wearing a minimum of diamond jewellery, lugging a toddler. With her was a dark man, pockmarked face, presumably her husband. Before she could turn away, Pinky caught her eye. Kalai could tell that she wanted to turn away too, but it was too late.

They walked towards each other with wavering smiles, exchanged some inane pleasantries. Kalai was suddenly conscious of her yellow chiffon sari, big costume jewellery, brash laugh, pink lipstick.

'And how is Anju after all these years?' asked Pinky.

'Unchanged.'

But Kalai would not ask after Pinky's parents or her obviously wealthy husband or her snivelling brat. She stuck to describing how busy her shooting schedule was. 'You must go and see the new movie,' she urged Pinky, speaking with a sneer, which had pleased her afterwards for a long time. It still pleased her.

'Stop smiling and go to sleep,' said Anju. She turned off the light by the bedstead. 'You have to get up in time tomorrow to be married. I'll wake you at four.'

Kalai crushed a pillow under her neck and shut her eyes. Pinky had been trying to be nice, well bred. But why should *she* be all that? Kalai was proud of what she was doing, of who she had become. And she had no regrets about her new life, beginning tomorrow. There would be photos of her and Shekar in all the weeklies. Pinky could sigh over how dazzling they looked. If Pinky liked holidaying with her family in Manali, she could read all about Kalai and Shekar honeymooning in Switzerland.

Anju had nearly had a stroke when she told her where they were going to honeymoon. Even Shekar's parents had thought it was excessive. But Kalai wanted to show them. Show PKB. Show Pinky. Show the world. And yet . . .

As she drifted off, she wondered what glamorous political greybeard PKB was out romancing.

~

The priest thrust her hand on to Shekar's. 'Exchange rings,' he said.

She slid a big gold ring with a coin-shaped face etched with the image of Murugan on to Shekar's right hand ring finger. Then Shekar attempted to insert her own ruby ring on her finger, but it would not go beyond the second joint. It had fit well enough in the jewellery shop. It must have shrunk in the meantime. Or else her finger had grown fatter.

'My left hand ring finger is thinner,' she said to the priest. 'Shall we try that one?'

'No, no,' said the priest, briskly tapping his cheeks to remove the inauspiciousness brought about by her thoughtless suggestion. 'It is the bad hand,' he said. 'Let it stay here for now.'

So the ring stayed halfway up her right hand finger. Then the priest urged them to hold, together, the coconut upon which rested the 'thaali'. Kalai had never paid attention to it before, although it hung from every married woman's neck. A lump of gold in the shape of a big-breasted, pregnant sprite. It was strung on to a cotton thread smeared in turmeric, wound around the coconut smothered in vermilion and marigolds. The priest commenced a medley of chants to imbue the thaali with powers to prolong Shekar's natural life. More specifically, he implored the thaali to imbue Kalai, with its constant presence upon her person, with the power to make Shekar's life last beyond her own.

Shekar coughed as the smoke from the sacrificial fire swirled up. He was in the middle of parroting mantras after the priest. She held her handkerchief to her nose to hide a smile. The priest recited, 'Mangalyam thanthunane . . .' Shekar went, 'cough cough mami . . .'

Suddenly, a commotion broke out at the entrance of the wedding hall. The band stopped playing. The priest stopped chanting and waved at the band to carry on. People were standing up, making way. PKB stormed through the guests, flanked by a dozen politicos, all in blazing white silk shirts and veshtis. Then he was before them. He wore sunglasses. She couldn't see his eyes. She could not remember her anger. She bowed her head. She saw from the edge of her vision PKB thrusting his hand into his kurta pocket and bringing out a handful of rose petals. He scattered them over her and Shekar. Petals landed like soft breaths on her head.

'Keep well,' he growled through his afflicted throat.

She looked up and opened her mouth to voice her thanks, but the words would not come. He did not once look at her hero, only at her. Then he swept away and out with his entourage.

The entire place seemed calm as a flat, windless ocean.

'Erm erm,' said Shekar to the head priest, who gazed after PKB's exit with his mouth slack. 'Shall we continue?'

Kalai gave Shekar a wry grin.

He grinned back, but there was an uncertainty in his face, about his place in the scheme of things. She winked at him, to a flurry of titters from the aunts. Shekar laughed, certain again of her love. And she did love him, with all her heart. Yet she looked in the direction PKB left, perchance he was rushing back.

'Drum harder, drum harder,' shouted the priest to the band across the wedding hall. It was the cue for the big moment. Everyone got up and crowded around the stage. The priest lifted the thaali by its thread ends and gave it to Shekar. The pee pees screeched and the dum dums thundered. Shekar took the thaali to Kalai's neck. Her head was pushed down from behind by an aunt. Her thick flower-twined plait at the nape was lifted. Shekar tied the first knot. An aunt tied the second and third knots. Rice rained upon them. Not rose petals. No one ever threw rose petals on marrying couples. PKB's voice, as he blessed them, came back to Kalai with startling clarity. 'Keep well.' 'Nalla iru.' He slurred his las and ras. And Tamil was a language of ras and las. It was a miracle, they said, that he could speak again. The bullet still lodged in his throat, like an unwelcome guest, a permanent marriage. But he came, she thought, as her plait fell back on her nape and she was finally married. He came and he gave his blessings.

~

Later that afternoon, Kalai informed Anju that she and Shekar would go for a stroll on the beach. A couple of distantly related grannies sucked air in shock. And off they went from the house, footloose like escaped convicts with their leg irons cut. Free of the hundreds of people, free of the wedding saris and garlands and sandalwood–turmeric–vermilion on their faces and free of fifty kilos of jewellery. Kalai wore a light cotton churidar. Shekar wore a kurta pyjama. They held hands and bought sundal to eat by the water.

They watched the crabs scurrying as dusk fell.

There was a screech behind them. They turned to see, all the way across the sand, a van, stickered all over with election posters. Flags of black and rose stuck out from all sides. A voice began blaring through the megaphone on its roof as it wound its slow way on Beach Road.

'PKB's party,' said Kalai.

There was only a month to go till the state elections. It was widely predicted that PKB would win in a landslide.

'You were there, weren't you,' said Shekar, 'when he was shot?'

'Yes.'

She could still hear the gunshot. Her ears had rung for a month.

She told Shekar about it. Some gossip magazine had quipped, 'Shooting at a Shooting'.

~

It happened in the middle of a kidnap scene with MTR, PKB's favourite villain. She was la-di-da-ing in the house. MTR sneaked in and made a grab for her. She screamed and ran around while MTR gave chase, grappled with and grabbed the pallu of her sari, pulled her to him. A heroine in distress always wore a sari. MTR taunted her with his trademark rasping voice. The director kept looking at his watch. It was nearly seven o'clock on Christmas Eve, 1967. The director, a Catholic, seemed keen to finish the shoot for the day and go home.

PKB materialised, of course, and punched MTR twice. Kalai leapt away. MTR pulled a gun. Now PKB and MTR sprang apart. They circled each other around the periphery of the room. MTR gnashed his teeth. PKB narrowed his eyes and brought his arms up for a grab. MTR aimed. PKB looked alarmed. Kalai, with another scream, leapt in front of PKB.

The gun fired.

Strange, she thought, that she should hear it. She was being thrust away from PKB. There was a terrible, fleshy noise close to her ears. PKB's hands were gripping her shoulders rigidly, for some reason much longer than they ought to have been gripping her. There were screams, although, with her ears ringing so, it was impossible that she should hear them or remember hearing them.

~

'Awful,' said Shekar, now, kissing her fingers. 'Awful,' he repeated.

She did not tell Shekar that there was a smell like the burnt firecrackers from Deepavali. PKB's hands had to be pried from her shoulders. When she could finally turn around, she saw the pool of blood forming under him. Horrific sounds came from his throat, like water gurgling in a drain. She could not tell that to Shekar.

Nobody could say how the prop gun metamorphosed into a real gun with bullets. MTR protested innocence. The police arrested him, then released him for lack of sufficient motive. The film industry closed ranks. Was there any political motive? No one could tell. Everyone loved PKB within the party. There were high hopes for him.

She said to Shekar, 'After three days of suspense, he was declared out of danger, and they found his voicebox damaged. He could only croak.'

'Poor man,' said Shekar.

'So does this mean you are going to vote for him?'

'I like the other guy.'

She slapped his hands away in playful admonishment.

The other guy was the Speechwriter, leader of the Justice for Dravidians Party. Nobody could prove any connection between MTR and the Speechwriter. None of it made any sense.

'But who did it?'

'I once broached the subject with PKB,' she said to Shekar. 'But the hunt to find the mastermind behind the shooting came to nothing.'

~

A month after PKB was discharged from hospital, Ilango drove her to PKB's beach house in Mahabalipuram. It was a balmy evening. The sea breeze enveloped her as she went up the steps to the house. There was nobody around. Ilango stayed with the car. She knocked on the door. PKB opened it himself. He looked, for the first time to her, as old as he was. A bandage covered his neck completely. He had just had a second operation.

They sat by a window that faced the sea. They sat smiling at each other for some time. Then PKB took a small notebook from his pocket and wrote something in it. He held it up. Kalai bent forward to read it. His handwriting was unreadable. Like crazy scrawling ants. She peered for nearly a minute before she made out the words. 'The green sari suits you.'

It was the closest he had ever come to saying, 'You look beautiful.'

Kalai, knowing the weight behind his inane words, nearly cried. She still couldn't speak. Then he wrote again and, already, she could read his hand better.

'Don't worry. I'll speak again in a month and we will finish the film.'

'You must find out who swapped the guns.'

He shrugged. That was the end of the matter. He never charged MTR or sought to find out who was behind the shooting. Various conspiracy theories abounded. MTR continued to act as the villain in PKB's films. He was considered innocent. If PKB could forgive him, everyone said, then who are we to hold a grudge?

~

'What are you thinking about?' asked Shekar now. She had been staring at the horizon.

'I love watching the waves crash on the shore,' she said.

'It is the reason I do not mind moving to Madras,' he said. 'The climate is awful, but there is the sea, and there is you.'

He put his arm around her.

'You are lucky,' she said.

'I am,' he said. 'Was it not PKB who took you away from me for so long?'

She shrugged.

'So when are you going to tell me what happened between the two of you?'

'Why we fell out?'

'Yes.'

'I suppose we got sick of each other. It was all too much.'

~

It all came to a head in the summer of 1972. They were shooting two movies at once. PKB was shooting three movies. PKB, who was never late, who prided himself on his punctuality, started coming late to the set. When he did come, it wasn't his cinema assistants flanking him, but his new political cronies. He was always in some discussion with them, wheeling and dealing between scenes, in the breaks.

It had got to the point where she was suffering from incessant stomach cramps. Ilango had come one morning to her room as she lay listless, in pain. He said, 'Do you know, baby, PKB has fired Murali?'

'Has he?' I am sick of hearing about PKB, she thought. I am sick of PKB. I feel like a prisoner. She was so surprised by these thoughts, by their vehemence, that she sprang up from the bed.

Ilango thought it was shock from the news, and stood there gratified, chirping about the unfairness of the dismissal. Murali had done nothing, he insisted. Nothing at all. Kalai sent him to get the car ready. She had to shoot her scenes, after all.

Preying on her mind was not just the discontent in her stomach, but also the discontent with her situation in life. All the years since she started her acting career trailered past. After *People's Champion*, it had happened, somehow, that dates never worked out for her to accept any other movies apart from PKB's. Always, the call sheets clashed, or the script wasn't right, or she didn't like the director or hero or the second heroine. PKB said she ought to shine singly as the central and only heroine in her movies. But she did two, no three films with him where he had a second heroine, even a song or two with her. Granted, the other heroine always died and PKB only ended up happily married to Kalai. Why was it OK to have other heroines in his films, and not hers? And every year, if he made one or two films with her, he made one or two films without her as well. With another leading lady. The fish-eyed one. Or the square-faced one. The schedule, for him, didn't clash. Why had she not seen it before?

There was PKB, strolling on to the set like he had all the time in the world. She saw him with new eyes. The make-up cracking over his wrinkles, his throat like an old man's, shadows under his eyes the concealer could not conceal. His eyes, themselves, small and sunken. No amount of pancake could return to them that clarity and youth. He'd caught her eyes going to his throat. He picked up a cowboy bandana from a chair, tied it like a scarf around his neck. They shot a song.

Along the street, which was what the set was made to look like, Kalai led two girls in song and dance around PKB as he slowly advanced. No one had told her where he was coming from and where he was going. She had to mouth the lines 'May you prosper, for the poor to prosper. May you rule, for all to be well.' The lines disgusted her.

PKB stopped smiling humbly and motioned to the director to cut the filming. 'Give it some heart, Kalai,' he told her.

Her anger then reached her tongue. 'The director thought it was fine,' she said.

The whole set hushed. She looked at the director. He said, 'What PKB sir says is–'

She interrupted him. 'He has a mouth and I have ears. You don't have to play mouthpiece.'

She turned to PKB. 'This is a silly song,' she told him. 'It is trite, too obvious. You may as well stand up on a podium and say, "I'm contesting in the forthcoming elections. Vote for me." What is the need for song and dance? Or a story?'

'What is wrong with the story?' rasped PKB.

'There *is* no story,' said Kalai. 'You are a do-gooder. That is the whole movie. You barely even beat up the villains. You give them a speech and they become good guys and fall at your feet. You feed the poor. You walk on the street singing about the freedom fighters and hundreds walk behind you giving chorus. You come to a ditch and a man prostrates himself in the shit so your feet don't get sullied. What sort of cinema is this?'

'Anyone can make a film,' said PKB. 'What I am doing is making use of the medium for a greater good. For the greater public good.'

Then Kalai said the unforgivable thing. 'It will be simpler to shoot the CM in the throat and take his place.'

It came from nowhere. It wasn't clever. It was unkind. A childish taunt. She was appalled by her own words.

PKB went and sat down. Kalai pleaded a headache to the director and went home. The next day, PKB arrived on time and shot all his scenes with Kalai. And the day after.

And the next. There were not many retakes. They did not say a word to each other, except in dialogue.

When it was over, Kalai put the word out that she would act with other heroes. The day she got the offer of the movie that paired her with Shekar was the day PKB demanded an accounting of the party funds from the CM in a public meeting, which led to the split in the party.

~

'I'm still going to vote for the other guy,' said Shekar, as they left the beach. They stood on the pavement and shook the sand from their slippers.

'Don't tell Anju that,' she told him. They strolled homeward, passed a bajji stall. The smell of frying besan was too much to resist. Kalai bought chilli bajji, onion bajji and plantain bajji. Every variety available.

It was only when eating her fifth bajji that she realised stuffing herself was a way of mourning the end of PKB in her life. Mourning, also, the end of her acting career. She hadn't known before that she was one of those people who ate to feel better about something. Still, she thought, as she offered the last bajji to Shekar and, when he declined, began eating it herself, it tasted good.

~

Breaking tradition, they spent their wedding night at Kalai's home. Shekar's family home was in Bangalore, and their flight to Switzerland would leave from Madras International.

Over breakfast the next morning, Anju said to Kalai, 'I will send Ilango to cancel this silly press meet if you say the word.'

'There is no Ilango now.'

'You do not want everyone to speculate on your looks this morning, do you?'

It was embarrassing to hear such things from Anju.

'All they ever do is speculate and gossip. It's no different from any other day in my acting life.'

They were speaking in Tamil. Shekar spoke Tamil with an accent, and he mixed up words sometimes. This led Anju to believe he could not understand them when they spoke their good Tamil.

'Eat? Good food?' she now said to him, using babyish, pidgin words.

'Good, good,' he said, playing along, rolling his eyes and nodding in an exaggerated fashion, and helped himself to another vadai before the maid could leap in to serve him.

'All I'm saying is,' Anju said to Kalai, 'think of how people will talk. If you are going to swan off to Switzerland, when good old Kashmir would have done as well, you could at least be modest about it, not announce it to the press. And you don't want to be answering questions about "you know who" with your new him right beside you. It will get ugly and out of hand.'

'Are you worried about aspersions on my character, mother?' Kalai said sweetly.

'Not as such,' began Anju, but Kalai cut in.

'Then you should never have got me into this business, should you?'

'There's that blame again,' spat Anju. She dashed water from a tumbler on to her hand over the uneaten pongal.

'And this won't be the last time you hear of it,' said Kalai.

'I give up,' said Anju. She looked wistfully over at Shekar, and loaded another vadai on to his plate before he could protest.

~

In the car, they held hands beneath the driver's line of vision in the rear-view mirror. If he had been Ilango, it wouldn't have been necessary to show such propriety.

She had, in fact, shouted twice for Ilango that morning, while waiting for her coffee, and then wondered why this other man hovered sheepishly at the doorway.

'Ah, sorry, Pazhani,' she had said to him, feeling such grief, as though a friend had died, when she should be so happy.

But Pazhani said, 'It's no problem, madam. I'll get the car ready.'

He was a good man. And already, she was a 'madam'. Not 'baby' any more. Her life was hinging on a new phase. PKB and Ilango were gone, as if dead, the way Pinky and her school friends had gone. They had been ever-present in her life. Now, she thought, sitting at the vanity, there was Shekar. As she thought of him, he appeared and kissed her on the forehead, as though she were a child, or at least a child in the English films she so rarely saw nowadays.

Here in the car, she felt positive about the press conference. She couldn't start her new life, her honeymoon, without putting a full stop to her old one. You couldn't begin a new sentence without putting a full stop after the old sentence. The press conference was the full stop.

'You know,' said Shekar, examining her fingers, 'I understood, a bit, what you and your mother were talking about. My Tamil isn't so bad.'

'I know it isn't,' she said.

He was sweet and pure and miraculously innocent in spite of the whole corrupting influence of the cinema world. She adored him.

'How did we meet?' she said.

'In a dream.'

'No, we met on set.'

'Twice.'

She laughed. 'Both times I was meeting you for the first time.'

'You were, yes. You had forgotten me completely.' Brazenly, he put her fingers in his mouth.

The name that had seemed oddly familiar when the director mentioned it connected with his face. It all came back to her: their first film, *White Sari*, the embarrassing real-life bedroom scene.

She didn't know where to look except at him, and he was looking at her as though he had expected her, at that very moment, to walk through the door. To her knowledge he had never made another Tamil film after *White Sari*. She remembered their thwarted romance as she went to him, and she couldn't help feeling joy, for he wore his heart on his sleeve.

He said, 'Kalai Arasi, I'd been hoping you and I would meet again.'

'Then why didn't you do something about it before now?'

He raised and dropped a shoulder. 'I hoped,' he said, 'and we meet.'

~

She pulled her hand from Shekar's when the first question was asked. It was the old hound from *Kalki*. 'How does it feel to be married, Miss Kalai? I mean, Mrs Shekar.'

How did she feel? There was a mike in front of them, and a big vase of Ooty roses. Kalai pulled on her sari to improve modesty. It was white, with a green and silver border. She had chosen white to give herself an aura of just-married bliss. Shekar wore white too, to match her.

'It feels wonderful,' she said. 'I am now complete. Admittedly, one has to become used to the change of name.'

And so on. Banal, but necessary questions and answers, to establish her new life. Comments on the wedding sari, the jewellery. Was there any dowry? Certainly not. Will she look after her in-laws? No. The in-laws will remain in Bangalore. She wondered when they would get around to PKB, her only hero for nearly ten years. They didn't.

When for the third time there was a question about the

mixed Tamil and Kannada traditions in the ceremonies, she said, 'Don't you want to ask something more interesting than that? Don't you want to know how we met? Where we are going for our honeymoon?'

'So tell us, tell us,' they said.

But they did not want to know. Fuddy-duddy Tamils, she thought. They would vivisect the silly, superstitious rituals, but not really care about the heart of things. What did she and Shekar see in each other? What were their ideas for the future? Was there great love, great passion, great tenderness?

Finally, almost reluctantly, someone asked the jackpot question. 'Will you stop acting after your marriage, Miss Kalai?'

Mrs Shekar didn't stick even till the end of the press meet. She knew then that she'd always be Miss Kalai to them. She looked at Shekar, crisp and handsome in his white shirt, and smiled, as though to soothe him.

'Yes,' she told them.

No one reacted. They just sat scribbling under the noisy fans. They had expected a 'yes'. It was de rigueur. They would never give leading roles to a married woman anyway. Even if she was only twenty-five, they would give her mother-of-the-hero roles, and that too only if they took pity on her. They would even cast her as the mother of a hero she had paired with. There was that actress, Angamma, who was not yet thirty, and already she was the favourite movie mother of PKB. Kalai would never degrade herself that way.

'I will finish any outstanding commitments,' she said, although she had finished the final dubbing work on her last movie weeks ago. 'And I will then dedicate myself to my marriage.' Her triumph. Her dream. Having dinner every day with her hero. Waving goodbye each morning, stethoscope around her shoulders. Well, there wouldn't be a stethoscope. Handbag and bun, instead. Off to the ladies' club for some charity work. Kitty parties. Card games. Cutting ribbons.

'And I,' said Shekar, in a soft, false voice, 'will continue making films after my marriage.'

They warmed to him. This Kannada usurper of their Tamil princess. They asked him questions about his move to Madras. He flattered them.

'Madras,' he said, 'is the centre of the country's film industry. Even Hindi movies are mostly shot in Madras studios. So, of course, it makes sense to move here.'

There were one or two claps from the reporters.

'Besides,' he continued, 'they don't make masala dosais like they do in Madras. Not to mention jasmine idlis.'

There was a good round of applause for such sentiment. He was forgiven for marrying Kalai.

The conference wound down. The news of their going to Switzerland was noted and there was no comment. Eyes wandered towards the side tables where rows of sweets and souvenirs waited.

'OK,' said Kalai. 'Thank you all very much for coming. Do not forget the little mementoes before you go.'

'One last question, madam,' piped a voice. It was a new young face. The old hands knew that you called leading ladies 'miss', not 'madam'. He was scribbling in his notepad even as he put the question. 'There is a rumour that your assistant, Ilango, wasn't too happy with the situation. Your marriage. Could you enlighten us?'

'Did he tell you he wasn't happy?'

'They say he left his job and is now nowhere to be found.'

This was not the kind of bombshell Kalai was expecting. She thought there would be questions about her falling out with PKB. It was as though they were all dampened in enthusiasm by some gagging order. Only this untrained cub had the lack of wisdom to posit wild speculations about someone of no account (to anyone but herself) like Ilango.

'Where did you hear this?' asked Shekar.

The boy moved his feet, looking uneasy. 'As I said, there is a rumour.'

'I have to disappoint you,' said Kalai, 'but the simple fact is, Ilango has jaundice. I'm sure you know what kind of illness that is. He has gone to his native village to rest and recover.'

The balloon that was the young reporter punctured with her reply. His chubby, irritating face deflated.

That wasn't the end of it. Someone else piped up: 'One last question, Miss Kalai.' And here it is, she thought. PKB.

'Whom will you vote for in the coming legislative elections?'

She realised why the questions were so tame. PKB was a saint. They wouldn't ask a single question that cast aspersions on his moral character. All the reporters, like all the masses, worshipped PKB.

The man repeated his question.

She had nothing to hide. She was all truth and plainspeak. 'For the incumbent CM,' she said, and got up to thank them once again.

2005

Jyoti was out ferreting for titbits from 6 a.m. His editor at the *Daily Pearl* had called him in just as he was leaving for home the previous evening, and asked him to cover the wedding procession. The editor had added, caustically, 'There is no need for any digging.' But there were some habits one could not break.

Jyoti liked the morning ride on his TVS Scooty. The clean sea winds on his face, unpolluted yet by the farting, belching humanity, unheated yet by the always angry sun. There was a purity of thought and purpose in the early morning. A keenness of spirit. A quickness of mind. He could get ten things done between 5 and 7 a.m., and struggle with one thing for the rest of the day.

Jyoti puttered behind a bus, no doubt full of fish and vegetable sellers, not remotely feeling the urge to overtake. Some habits one wouldn't break.

Serene in traffic, he was a bloodhound in his job. Jyoti considered his school or style to be investigative journalism, not Page Three society reporting, no matter how the trend in news content and marketing changed. He would go to his deathbed, poor but proud, as the reporter who gave it everything and, in his time, exposed one or two wrongdoers in high office, and got not kudos for it, only sticks. He simply wanted to be able to face himself (bearded, buck-toothed and foolish-looking) in the mirror every morning, and face his wife, behind him with the towel, who had principles, and had refused to marry a man settled abroad like all her sisters. A journalist, she liked to tell him, is the highest patriot.

He rode on to the Marina. Normally, the narrow Santhome Road would widen into Beach Road, the beach would come into view, the sky would lift up and alles clair, as the Germans said. Now, blocking even the wide expanses of the beach and parts of the sky were big cut-outs of the CM, the bride and the groom. Strung between the lamp posts, straddling sky and earth. Workmen were erecting some pillar-like contraptions all along the road.

He stopped his TVS just beyond the All India Radio building. He didn't bother locking it. A thief wouldn't dare steal from the vicinity of a political event. Jyoti could be a party worker, in spite of his beard, his khadi kurta and jeans. And party workers, white-shod or not, were sharks that ate up petty thieves like minnows.

Jyoti took his pad out and approached a man who was hoisting up a papier mâché pillar all on his own. He waited for the man to finish. The pillar was a white, garish thing, botched up in some movie industry workshop where they made props for mythological films. It belonged in a low-budget Indraprastha or Indraloga. The pillar next up was already hoisted, and a crow sat screeching on top. Another man came running to shoo it away. The crow didn't deign to notice, just streamed its shit.

The man hoisting the pillar with his two bare hands grunted, tottered and nearly collapsed with the weight, before suddenly, with a stunning grin of effort, pushing it upright. Jyoti waited with his pen on paper.

The man finished panting, and said to Jyoti, 'You a journalist?'

'Yes.'

'You look like something from them movies, you know, a movie journalist. Always getting murdered.' The man laughed. The burden of the pillar had fallen from his shoulders, just like that.

If only all jobs were that simple, thought Jyoti. That clear-cut.

'People tell me that,' said Jyoti, with a slight smile. 'What is your name?'

'I'm your source, aren't I?' said the man, cagily. 'I won't tell you my name. You can give me, what is that called, a nickname. Pseudonym,' he added in English.

'How long have you been working here?'

'Give me a nickname first.' The man sat down on the road and fanned himself.

'Mmm, how about "The Teller"?'

'I like "Light of the Truth" better.'

'OK, Light of the Truth, tell me about your work here.'

'I am, what is it called, casual labour. I come at midnight with the others, in the lorry. They promise good pay.' He held up two fingers for a second before taking them to scratch the top of his ear. 'We should be finished by now, but it will take at least till four o'clock.'

'This afternoon?'

'Yes.'

'Why, what more needs doing?'

'These pillars, you see, are all lamps. They need wiring, bulbs, and all should work. Every single one of them, otherwise she will have your head.' He seemed quite cheerful about it. He grinned.

'That is not your job, I presume.'

'No, no, the electricians will come by later. I only put things up. Construction-like.'

'What else do you need to put up?'

'Oh, all sorts. More banners, whatnot, speakers. Flowers. They will all be coming down with the things. From the head office.'

'From the party head office?'

'No, your grandma's head office. What are you, simple?'

'And you get two hundred rupees?'

'Who knows? The leaderess might be pleased and give us an extra tenner?' Light of the Truth laughed at his own joke, stood up, dusted off his backside and went on to hoist the next light pillar.

Supplies frm party hq? Jyoti wrote in his notepad. *Party org for a pvt ceremony? & w. abt permissions, etc, for tk over arterial rd o. t. city?*

Cd pvt ind do tht sort of thing? If supplies & labour are org by party hq, where is the money coming from? Two hundred multiplied by hundreds, just to start with. Is it coming from party funds? As always, he couldn't sustain his homemade shorthand.

He noted that the cut-outs of the CM were more numerous than those of the bride and groom. All the colours of the banners were black, rose and white, which would indicate, he thought, that the party was involved. But he would keep an open mind.

Appearances could not be used to draw too many inferences. *Solid proof,* he wrote and underlined.

~

Kalai Arasi touched the bride's bent head. 'May you live long and die a married woman,' she said, blessing the bride. A chit of a girl. Twenty years old. The groom helped the girl into the wedding carriage. A real carriage, like the British of old, decorated with red and white flowers. Black was inauspicious. The groom had to squeeze into the carriage. He used to be a thin boy, sprightly, smart, with a lot of promise. Now he was chubby. He was going into the family business. Real estate. The stench of money.

Kalai climbed into a decorated car behind the carriage, next to Selvi. Selvi was all red. Kalai was all green. That was the only difference. She had allowed herself to be persuaded, yet again, to dress like her best friend. Same design of silk sari. Gold enough to keep a Lakshmi deity in a temple happy.

The procession started. Lights, diffused through the material of paper pillars all along Beach Road, threw the scenery into a mirage. It was as though the ocean had stolen in while their heads were turned away, crept up and over them. Now they were all underwater. Even the sounds came diffused, soft somehow, in a land where sound was never soft. She was sitting in a decorated open car in a marriage procession which was a surreal affair, nothing like anybody had ever seen in their lives, and she felt the weight of the water over her, all over her, pressing gently like the jewellery upon her.

The wedding band started playing movie songs. The carriage and her car rolled at walking pace. The wedding guests, all Selvi's relatives, walked with them. Was it her idea, to parade like this in the middle of the city? Why did she adopt the groom? She always thought of him as Shekar, but his name was something else. She could not remember it. Selvi's nephew, the boy she had admired, the boy she had thought, so many years ago, could have been hers and Shekar's, if Shekar's genes had dominated. What had her so deluded? He was now, what, twenty-four? Nothing like Shekar. He looked like Selvi. Dark, fat, constantly sweaty, already balding. They were all fat.

A photographer came close to the carriage.

'Smile please,' Kalai heard him say to the bride. The bride sat as though cowed from birth. She reminded Kalai of someone. Some actress. Oh yes, her co-heroine in her very first film, *White Sari*. What was her name? The bride looked younger than her twenty years. Kalai knew the girl would be pregnant in a month, gain weight in three, and never lose it again.

The same photographer approached the car. He put his camera to his face and adjusted focus, walking slowly backwards to keep them in shot. For a moment, Kalai thought he was going to say, 'Smile please' to her, but he didn't.

She must appoint a dietician, a nutritionist, whatever one called them nowadays. She could afford three. Officially her salary was one rupee a month, as she had declared to great fanfare two years ago, but she could afford anything. She didn't have to lift a finger and money poured in. A person in power, she thought, attracted and accumulated wealth, like a sickly person attracted and accumulated diseases.

'A feast awaits us when we get to the wedding hall,' Selvi whispered, leaning over. 'I hired the Taj chef.' She looked gleeful, like an overgrown little girl, spilling her blouse, full of mischief.

Kalai could think of no one else she'd rather do these things for, or in this case, *allow* these things for. But she was getting fat. They were getting fat together.

~

At least five kg of gold on each, wrote Jyoti in his pad. *CM's salary 1 re p m. What abt frnd? What does frnd hub mk? How?*

Jyoti wrote as he walked behind the wedding carriage, trying not to step on the toes of any wedding guest in the melee. He wondered if some of them were part of the CM's family. They chatted in low tones. Most of them had a Thanjavur accent. He could catch a few phrases, meaningless to him. 'Thalaivi' was the word that pinged from several mouths. Leaderess. Did she not set aside her own family, all her old acquaintances? The lonely lioness on top of the food chain. Was there anyone else whom the word Thalaivi suited more? In Tamil, there were separate words for male and female leader. Thalaivan, PKB. Thalaivi, Kalai Arasi. Of course, in Tamil, the words also meant hero and heroine, of literature, of the movies. *Is that why movie actors transitioned so smoothly into politics?* He scribbled furiously, forgetting again the shorthand in his hurry to keep up with his train of thought. *Is that why Tamils are peculiarly prone to entrusting their lives to protagonists of make-believe? Is it all down to word confusion?*

The sun had set just a moment ago and the sky was an immodest pink. But not as immodest as some of the women inside the security cordon. The weight of silver and gold, silk and gems, would sink a good ship or two.

His distaste grew as he became aware of the sheer scale of the procession. Blocking off two arterial roads in the city at rush hour, causing five-hour jams all the way through the rest of the city, like blood clots in a heart. Such pomp, such parade, such wealth. While half the population was starving. And surprisingly for Tamils, the desire to show off. This, indeed, was new.

Journalists and photographers were encouraged to walk with the procession. No limits on photos, just no questions, please. The friend of the leaderess even turned to wave at the flashing bulbs from time to time, as though she were the English Queen.

'Ssss.'

He had stepped on the toe of another journo. From *The Times*.

'Hey,' he said. 'Sorry. Sorry.'

'It's OK,' said the *Times*. Jyoti knew him vaguely. Page Three society. Jeans, tucked-in shirt, clean-shaven. Still looking like a college boy.

'Hey, I know you,' said the *Times*. 'Grew up reading your stories.'

Jyoti winced. Then smiled to be polite.

'I've finally caught up with you,' said the *Times*.

No, thought Jyoti, I've tumbled down to your level, at last, for there is nothing left up there. He didn't say anything.

'Do you know,' said the *Times*, in a whisper, '. . . peacock throne?' Jyoti could hardly hear him in all the noise of the band and the chatter and cameras.

From history, thought Jyoti. Some Mughal, was it, and his peacock throne? Didn't the British steal it?

'The bride and groom,' said the *Times*, 'will be seated, at the end of the procession, on a golden peacock throne. I have the exclusive inside info. I thought I would give you a lead, so you have twenty minutes before the others find out. I have the maker's details, and he is giving me an interview, but I won't give you that.'

'No problem. Thanks,' said Jyoti.

As he walked he penned a lead in his head. *This reporter attended what was a private wedding procession, but it could have easily been mistaken for a vast public event, one of even national importance, given the scale and pomp. Few republic day parades could match it in grandeur, but a few movies can. The drums song in* Chandralekha, *for example, if there are those still alive who remember such a movie.*

The procession was ugly. The cut-outs and decorations and the papier mâché lamps were all ugly. The entire clan of the leaderess's friend were ugly. He could not remain neutral about it, no matter how hard he tried.

He continued the report in his head, even though he knew it to be a futile exercise. *Let me now present to you a series of questions. I shall not presume anything. I shall merely present to you what I have seen and heard, and you can make up your own minds as to what it all means . . .*

Suddenly, a pee-pee blared close to his ear. Blindly, he had walked to the side of the wedding band, and was caught up in their tasteless thunderings. He hung back, let the band pass. He really did not want to see the peacock throne, but he had to, to be able to describe it accurately to all the millions in the state who did not have the same privilege, and who were probably paying for it, one way or another.

Ah, there he went again, being polemical. No, he would simply present facts and questions, like a true reporter. He would leave the conclusions to the readers.

Jyoti heaved a sigh. They had reached the wedding hall. He queued for the banquet. He was starving. He hadn't eaten since six that morning. All for what? Who was he kidding? Nothing he wrote would be printed. The editor would send it back, and ask for a straightforward report

of the wedding. In a hundred words or less. Jyoti had to
do it his way first. The editor wasn't a bad man. He just
didn't want party hooligans thrashing his office, breaking
equipment. He didn't want to be jailed for slander and
beaten up in the cells. He didn't want acid thrown on his
wife's face. Jyoti didn't want that either. But he couldn't
change his habits. No more than an old, crippled leopard
could change its spots.

~

Under the canopy of a neem tree, suffused with the
pleasure of having just opened the hundredth women-
only police station – numerous speechifiers had declared
it her greatest legacy – Kalai Arasi, with just Selvi and a
few of her favourite ministers, sat down to her birthday
banquet. They were at Woodlands restaurant. Ever since
she married Shekar, she had come here for her birthday
lunch. After Shekar died, she came with Anju. After Anju
died, with Selvi. Over the course of her rule, she could not
fathom how the ministers, she counted fifteen of them,
came to join her.

On the table were her favourite tiffin items. Masala
dosais, pongal, upma. Idlis with coconut chutney.

Manikavel was saying, 'Very simple, madam. This is
what the people love about you. Others go to five-star
hotels to celebrate their birthdays. You come to Woodlands.
Middle-class institution.'

She looked at him. His eyes the size of the thayir

vadais on the table. He would be all praise, wouldn't he, she thought. The high court had just acquitted him of all charges in the building scam lawsuit.

Selvi, beside her, said through a mouthful of masala vadai, 'Yes, yes, even the Superstar only goes to Chola Rooftop. Kalai madam is content with Woodlands.'

'Does he?' said Kalai, surprised at this bit of intimate information about such a public figure as Superstar Sathya. Even though he was her contemporary in age, he had been a nobody when she was a star. Now he was at the peak of his cinema career, romancing sixteen-year-olds in a wig and dungarees.

Vairam, a new minister in the fold, rings on all ten fingers gleaming, bent over another man to say, 'The Superstar, he goes after the Rooftop closes. Midnight. The staff stay late to cook all his favourite dishes.'

'So pompous,' said Selvi.

'Making the staff stay late to cook him Chicken 65,' huffed Manikavel.

Kalai couldn't agree with them. Woodlands, after all, had to close for the whole day so she could lunch here. She had no choice. A CM wasn't like an ordinary clerk wanting Woodlands pongal. Selvi had insisted. Security reasons. They were compensated, of course.

The staff were milling around the perimeter established by her Black Cat security, craning for a glimpse from her. Every mouthful she ate they scrutinised, her face they read for its registering of taste, approval, disapproval. Indifference would be intolerable to them.

'It must be galling for Sathya,' she said, 'that everyone knows where he goes, and what he eats.'

'Price of fame,' Selvi said firmly.

The owner of Woodlands came with coffee.

'Special Mysore coffee I made myself, madam,' he said. A simple, unostentatious man.

She nodded towards the table. He found a space for it. A tumbler inverted inside a cup. The hot coffee held by a kind of pressure. She liked to flip the dabara upside down in one fluid motion, without spilling a drop. She reached for it. A car door slammed. Vijayan got out, sweating.

'Sorry, madam, couldn't wait. I got word of the front-page item in *Evening Rose*.'

Her hand trembled ever so slightly on the coffee dabara. The coffee came gushing out into the cup.

'And what is it about?' she said.

'It is an article written by a veteran *Daily Pearl* reporter, about the wedding.'

Pearl?

'Yes, madam. The *Pearl* editor refused to publish it. But somebody on the subediting desk, rumour says the Speechwriter's illegitimate son's brother-in-law, sent it to the *Rose*.'

'With the reporter's permission?'

'Erm, madam, the reporter is said to have suddenly left town.'

'Oh, and is his article damning?'

Vijayan looked stricken. The bearer of bad news didn't

want his head chopped off. 'Madam, I have here a copy. Pardon me.'

She pushed the coffee dabara away from her. It teetered near Manikavel's elbow. 'Never mind the whole article. Just give me the precis.'

'Madam,' Vijayan pleaded again. 'Forgive me. It is about how the wedding was extravagant and is costing the government millions. Public nuisance. Corruption, and so on and so forth. He has interviewed everyone from the suppliers to the construction workers. He has traced all the payments to party HQ. Even budgeted the whole thing.'

'Well, that will help the husband,' said Selvi. 'He has no head for budgeting.'

Kalai gave Selvi a look. How inappropriate her comment was. How blithe.

Kalai noticed that all the ministers were waiting for a response from her.

'When you have been leader of a party for so long,' she said, 'personal matters and party matters get mixed together, do they not?'

'Yes, madam,' one or two of them said in their best sycophantic voices.

'He has even described the jewellery worn by everyone,' said Vijayan, crestfallen. 'He seems to even know the carats of diamonds and rubies.'

Kalai felt her cheeks turn hot. Pretty stones, she thought. What did she know of the nature of gold and precious stones? The value of pretty things? It came to her for no good reason, Anju all those years ago, on that beach, telling her that all her jewellery was fake, had always been. She had been counting on the trinkets as an insurance against Anju.

How much gold and precious stones did it take to feel secure? How much property to put away for old age? How much money for when famine struck?

'Bring me the paper when it gets printed,' she said.

'But just stop them before they print it,' said Selvi.

'No. They can print what they like. The people have a right to make up their own minds.'

She asked for the finger bowl. 'I'm done here,' she said. 'Back to work.'

As if at a gunshot, the ministers flew to their cars, brisk and businesslike for her approval.

1985

Shekar's things lay everywhere. Kalai walked around the house, looking and touching. His VIP suitcase on top of the dresser. His clothes. Shirts still hung from hangers and trousers lay folded and stacked on shelves. He had stuck to his seventies styles well into the eighties. The shirts still had big collars, dizzying patterns. The trousers were elephant's legs. His towel hung in its place in the bathroom. His shaving brush and razor were on the washstand. His shoes and slippers were lined up next to hers in the shoe rack. The special Kannadiga podi he liked to eat with his idlis lay in a small steel box in the kitchen. His awards lined the display cases in the hall.

She opened a case and touched the silver and copper moulded front of an award. His third Cinefare Best Actor.

'Oh thank you, thank you, thank you,' she said to the award. He always said his thank yous thrice. She smiled the way she did when teasing him. Anju came into the room and stood next to her, looking at the awards.

'I asked Pushpa to get some nice mangoes from the market,' said Anju.

Kalai nodded. She shut the case.

'Why don't you go out, some ladies' club meeting, some party?'

'I have too much to do.'

'Like what?'

She did not have an answer. She wanted to be alone and think about the last ten years, perhaps. She had a lot of clearing up to do. Shekar's things. Put the house in order. Put her thoughts in order. She did not have time to go out, to worry about what to wear and how to do her hair and then go and compare saris and hairstyles and jewellery and husbands and children. She didn't have any children. She didn't have a husband any more.

Now there was only Anju, and who knew how long she was going to stick around? Probably forever, just to torment her.

'I need to pack up his things,' said Kalai.

'I'll help you fold his clothes,' said Anju. 'But leave the awards. I like looking at them.'

'Of course.'

Kalai pulled out all his clothes. Then she sat down on the floor with Anju to fold them. Anju was soft now, grandmotherly, though neither Kalai nor Ganesh had given her any grandchildren. Anju was happy being quiet and going about things in the house, walking to some temple every evening to get some air and talk to other older ladies. Her stinger had rotted and fallen off with age.

Kalai lingered over each shirt, each handkerchief. Anju too folded the clothes very slowly. Just when Kalai would find her presence a real comfort, Anju would die too. Kalai

would then be all alone with her thoughts and mementoes.
Like those useless awards.

~

Later, when Kalai was finally done with packing up all
of Shekar's things, she came out to find Anju skinning a
radish at the dining table.

'Pushpa put too much tamarind in the sambar yesterday,'
said Anju. 'I'll be making lunch today.'

In the early days of her marriage, when Anju visited
Kalai's in-laws in Bangalore, she took offence to their way
of putting coconut and jaggery in the sambar. Her poor
mother-in-law caught on only much later what made Anju
so sour in her behaviour, as if to counter the sweetness of
their Bangalore sambar. By the time her mother-in-law
gave the cook fresh instructions, it was too late to impress
Anju. Anju would not deign to visit her more than once a
year, and made a point of praising the correct preparation
of sambar each time she did visit. Her poor mother-in-law
would smile and nod nervously. She was dead too.

Kalai pulled up a chair opposite Anju.

'I'll make a nice tamarind sauce,' said Anju. 'Won't need
any poriyal, although I'll make one. A potato fry, perhaps.
Or cauliflower. But if you like, you can eat it just with the
mango.'

A rare treat. When Kalai was very young, very
occasionally, when she was recovering from a fever, and
if it was the right season, Anju would allow her to forgo

poriyal, and just eat curry and rice with mango.

'I'm not sick, Anju,' said Kalai, but she said it gently.

'No, but you are recovering,' said Anju.

~

That evening, Anju and Kalai watched a Tamil series about Alladin and his magic lamp. Alladin had been shut in an underground cave, and evil spirits came to sing a song of torment to him. Anju watched with her mouth slightly open. It was Anju's way to be completely immersed in whatever was on TV, be it advertisements, the news or simply the plaintive tune of Doordarshan that accompanied the pyschedelic swirls indicating there was no programming at the moment.

A bomb could go off right next to her, and she wouldn't notice. She didn't hear the shrill ringing of the phone. Instead of her usual irritation at Anju's lack of reaction, Kalai felt a small admiration. She wished she could shut out the world too, remain uninterrupted in her own thoughts, in her own home. Kalai ignored the phone. Whoever it was, she did not want to speak to them. It wasn't to be. The maid, Pushpa, came huffing and puffing to pick up the receiver.

'Alo . . . she is here . . . what should I say . . . she will call back . . . no she won't speak now . . . yes I'm sure . . . who am I? I'm your big sister . . . give me the message and your number . . . oh . . . oh . . . understand sir . . . yes . . . right away . . . I'll hang up now.'

The maid dropped the receiver back on the cradle and

sat abruptly on the floor. 'Oh, they are going to arrest me
for showing too much tongue. Oh you fat-headed woman
. . .' she wailed.

Kalai could not make head nor tail of what was going
on. 'Who was it, Pushpa?'

'His secretary, baby. His personal secretary. And I
thought he was some old fan as usual.'

'Whose secretary? You are acting like it was the PM.'

'Oh, it's not the PM. Who cares about some Hindi PM
sitting in Delhi and whether he calls or crawls. This is more
than the PM. It is our own CM!'

~

Chief Minister PKB had a smile on his face. Seated in
a large squishy armchair that seemed to engulf his frail
person, he also had the appearance of being swamped by his
woolly Kashmiri cap and oversize sunglasses. His formal
drawing room was vast, strewn with sofas and high-back
chairs of impeccable taste, large windows with reinforced
steel bars in the shapes of lotuses and elephants. There was
no one else in the room. The secretary who accompanied
Kalai from the front door, through the hallway and here,
withdrew, pulling the door curtains closed behind him.

'Arasi,' said PKB when she came near him, holding out
his hand, still sitting. Having expected him to jump up
and seize her by the shoulders with a cloud-splitting smile
and mirth-filled eyes, Kalai was disappointed that he
remained seated. That ridiculous hat and glasses did not

allow anyone to see the truth in his eyes or even the span of his head.

She took his hand, was surprised by how thin it had become.

'Sit, sit,' he said, 'close to me, so I don't have to shout.' His voice sounded worse than ever. All his public speeches lately, her mother had remarked, were short and punchy. What a far cry from the droning politicians. Anju said the people approved of leaders who were so busy doing the public a service they only had time to leap on the stage, give a thundering, passionate speech for a minute and leap off to get on with the business of serving the poor.

But this PKB here, with a voice so weak she could barely hear him, even sitting so close, could not be the same PKB creating a revolution in political speech-making, with his punchy, one-minute speeches.

'You know, I always thought you should be called Arasi, even though Kalai is a perfectly good name,' he said.

She could not bear it any more. She said, 'Do you have to sit here like a masked burglar?'

He laughed heartily, if weakly. 'Oh I completely forgot, my child,' he said, putting a hand up to feel his hat and glasses. 'I had Manikam visiting just before you, you know him?'

Kalai shook her head.

'The new MP, silly. You really should follow the news, you know, I keep telling you.'

'The last time you told me was ten years ago, actually.'

PKB laughed, removed his hat and glasses.

Kalai struggled to keep her composure. He looked like a little old man, but not a little old man like Gandhi, who, even in his eighties, was walking from Uttar Pradesh to Madhya Pradesh and keeping fast for weeks. PKB's eyes did not have the divine light any more that Tamil cinema audiences called the light of God. His cheeks, known for their romantic hero voluptuousness, were sunken. His lips were dry, his forehead ashen. He had a perfect half-moon of baldness on the top of his head. The few scraggly hairs behind were dyed jet black.

'Are you keeping well?' she asked.

'Yes, yes, of course. Never been better.'

'That's hard to believe.'

'Oh, you know, a cough and a fever now and then. Do you not want to know why I asked you to see me?'

Deathbed wish, she couldn't help thinking. But no, he wasn't quite at death's door.

'I thought you might have heard about Shekar,' she said. 'But for that, you would have come in person or sent word, not sent me a summons like I'm a lackey.' She smiled to soften the harshness of her words.

'Yes, I did hear, and you are right,' said PKB. 'I'm very sorry, Arasi. He was so young. And so good to you.'

'He was,' said Kalai, and there was nothing more to say about Shekar, even to PKB. He was good, and he was gone.

'But you are right,' continued PKB. 'I called you on business.'

'You aren't making another movie, are you?' said Kalai. 'I refuse to be your screen mother.'

They both laughed, and it was good to laugh with him. She could see the old PKB now, the one who had not completely morphed into Chief Minister.

'Curse this armchair,' he said, getting up awkwardly, one arm on the sofa for balance. 'I need my divan. Come with me.'

Kalai followed PKB to an interior room, which had a big desk and a divan to one side. He sat on the divan with his feet up, and Kalai helped pile some cushions behind him.

'So you want to know what I want from you.'

'Tell me,' she said. 'I am at your service.'

'I want you to campaign for me in the coming elections,' he said.

'Campaign?'

'You will be the party's official spokesperson. You will be the face of the party.'

'You are the face of the party.'

'I won't be here, you see, for a month or two. You have to campaign in my place. You must become my emissary to the people of Tamil Nadu. You must get them to re-elect me.'

She laughed. 'It isn't what I expected at all.'

'What did you expect, Arasi?'

'That you wanted me to read to you by your bedside every afternoon.'

Now he laughed. 'If things don't go well, I might come to that stage.'

'Where are you going?'

'I have to undergo a very minor operation. You know, the usual. Number thirty-one or thirty-two. I will be in Chicago for a month, two at the most.'

'You will be here in time to take your oath?'

'Of course. The good work must continue,' said PKB. 'But it won't without your help.'

'I cannot do it.'

'Why, have you got any other pressing engagements?'

'I am in mourning.'

'But I need you, Arasi. And you need a challenge. We are both alive, aren't we? And free as birds. I need your strength, your support.'

And so, for the second time in her life, Kalai said yes to PKB, when she meant to say no.

～

Kalai didn't feel nervous till the morning she had to leave from Madras. Pushpa opened the front door at six in the morning and ten politicos in white shirts and veshtis with black and rose borders stormed in, all in a froth.

Kalai, still in her nightie, hurriedly threw a towel over her shoulders.

'Why are you all here?' asked Kalai. 'Would one person not do?'

'We are all to go with you, for help and advice,' said the man who was half a foot taller and a span wider than the rest of them. 'We all accompany the CM on his campaign tours.'

So many, she thought. And all men.

'I will be five minutes,' she said to them.

She was a little intimidated. They looked rough and tough. She was used to the soft movie type of man. Like Shekar. A small needle turned in her flesh. The directors and actors. The dreamers. Ones who liked to laugh and joke. The boy-ladies. These men here, her new chaperons, were political minions – which really meant the criminal type who cut throats to shape careers. She wanted them outside. She didn't want them a minute longer in the house. She hurried into Anju's room and shook her awake.

'Come with me,' she said.

Anju lay prone and wide-eyed like a dead body. She seemed already aware of the activity in the house.

'I am too old to be running around with you,' she said.

'I know, but you just have to sit close. I would never ask you to run and fetch things,' said Kalai, with a small laugh. She was terrified to be leaving with all these strange men. Even though she knew that they wouldn't hurt a hair on her head. Or PKB would have something to say about it. But PKB was a frail old man, losing his voice and lying unconscious on an operating table in Chicago.

'You have to go on your own, baby,' said Anju. She closed her eyes.

It was like a slap. She hated her mother then, all over again. Anju had fooled her into loving her once more, lulled her into a sense of well-being, and now she pulled the mat from under her feet.

'Anju,' she said, 'there isn't a single woman coming with me.' She hated herself for begging.

Anju pretended to be asleep. In her impotent frustration, Kalai switched the fan off on the way out. Let Anju get up to turn it on again.

She packed a suitcase. Even in the male-dominated movie industry, there were always women around. The extras and the mother and sister characters, the make-up and hair women, the dance mistress and her assistants, the costume ladies. For all her aversion to female co-stars, she had always preferred female crew. When there was a male make-up artist, she usually ended up doing her own.

Strong as steel, she thought. Put metal in your mind. She would spend five minutes every day invoking an iron cage around her, which would keep the men at bay. Not a cage. Armour, like the knights of England. She stepped out with this armour around her and the ten burly men did not seem so intimidating.

Outside her front door, an Ambassador car with the back door open had its engine running. Pushpa was loading her luggage with the driver's help. Behind it were three more cars. Behind the cars, a lorry, and in the back, all standing, packed like bananas on a branch, were about two hundred men, staring at her in the morning silence.

~

They arrived, mid afternoon, at Karaikudi, the coastal fishing town.

'Is this it?' Kalai asked the man seated beside the driver, her appointed 'all-in-all' for the length of the campaign. She had expected a small stage at a small ground. But it was enormous.

'It is for the great leader,' said Maran. A burly man with bulging bloodshot eyes, he was like a movie thug. She wished she had someone smaller, sweeter, altogether more manageable.

She had asked them to drive past the stage on the way to the hotel. It was still early. She would rest, shower, eat, change, clear her throat a few times. There was time for all that.

'Will it be ready by evening?'

'Of course,' he said, as if she were silly to ask.

The stage was far from ready at the moment. Men banged away at the floor planks. Men erected poles on the corners. Men stood on ladders holding out the party bunting, lurid, distorted images of PKB and other party greats among them in swirls of black and rose. They tried to tie them to the tops of poles even before the poles were set straight. A few dozen chairs, for the more important of the audience, stood in desultory stacks. The vast unwashed would stand behind the few seated. The proletariat would be on its feet, PKB's fate in its collective callused hands, not knowing that he was nothing without them. But then the people were putty in PKB's own soft hands.

They reached the guest house. Kalai barely had time to wash her face, when Maran knocked on the door.

'I am here to help you prepare the speech,' he said.

'Oh, come in then,' she said.

They sat on tiny chairs, facing each other.

'You have to make them see PKB through you,' the big man told her. He scowled as if his own idea unfathomably annoyed him. And he was staring at her as if staring would miraculously transform her into PKB. Kalai had a headache.

'The trick is to see the thousands of people as one mass, one body,' said Maran, as if he was some debating coach. 'The ground may now look very big, but when it is filled by the people, it will look small, from the stage.'

He was irritating. And he was stupid.

'Well, surely only a few hundred people are going to turn up, Mr Maran.' She knew the Mr irked him. The goons preferred to be addressed as 'Anna'. Big brother. But no, she would keep the distance, thank you very much. She would be the westernised bitch. 'Even for my biggest public appearances, no more than five hundred turn up, and I retired ten years ago.'

Maran and his mustachios quivered a little, as he held her eyes, and the eyes bulged a little. Kalai held her breath, fearing assault.

'Sorry, madam,' he said. 'I should have told you earlier. They don't know that the CM is not coming.'

~

Kalai stood in front of the microphone in her plainest sari, with the barest of make-up. She shook the mike down to the level of her mouth. Behind the sharp curve and line of the mike, in blurry focus, heaved the vast entity that was the public.

Thousands of fishermen and women, waiting in pin-drop silence for her to begin. Behind her four politicos waited also, for their turn at the lectern. She was the first speaker.

They waited quietly. She gathered her thoughts and breath. There were no more than a few murmurs when the local MLA announced that PKB was not among them, that he had flown to some emergency meeting with the President of the United States. 'PKB himself has sent Miss Kalai Arasi in his place,' the man had said, moving his hands in a flourish towards her. To her surprise, there were claps. In the mad moment of silence that followed the MLA's announcement, she had expected the crowds to break out in chaos, climb the stage and assault them. She had always been given to believe that PKB threw his followers into a religious frenzy, that they knew neither rhyme nor reason in their devotion, that they were animals. But here they were, as polite as though at a cricket match, cheering the substitute.

She cleared her throat to begin, and the fear seized her. What was she going to say? She had her speech written down days ago, but it now seemed lame, fit for a current affairs school debate, not to persuade the masses to vote. Who was she? Why did they care what she had to say? Ultimately, she didn't care who they voted for, whether the state was ruled by this party or that. She had only ever voted once, only because she knew PKB personally. By the time the by-election came around in her ward, less than two years later, she had already lost interest.

She noticed a fisherman in the throng just behind the row of chairs. In the glare of the tube lights, his eyes and teeth shone. He was smiling, waiting. Around him, other men, in old but clean lungis, some bare-chested, probably straight from the boats, and others in their best, clean shirts, and women, so many women, not in their best saris, but second best, or third best, all stood there to be spoken to. They didn't seem to be frothing at the mouth with the frenzy of devotion to PKB. They seemed like sensible people. They were not a monstrous mass filling up the ground and making it shrink. They were just individuals. The wave of panic broke away. She began her speech.

'Vanakkam. I am here as a messenger from your beloved PKB, our dear Chief Minister, to persuade you to vote for him. I know that there is absolutely no need to persuade you all to vote for him, for you are reasonable people, and you would have already worked out that it is the most sensible thing to vote for him, a leader who will fight for a better life for you, rather than the opposition, who do not have the same devotion to you as does your current CM. Nevertheless, I would like to remind you of the reasons why "Progress for Dravidians" is a better choice than "Justice for Dravidians". Under our respected PKB, the PFD is dedicated to lift the people of Tamil Nadu out of poverty, to make sure that all the basic needs are met, that everybody prospers. Free lunch for schoolchildren, old-age pensions, ration rice at one rupee per kilo, these are but a few examples of the successful programmes introduced by our dear CM, and will continue to be implemented under his reign, if you vote for him. So I urge you, vote for the symbol of Coconut Frond.' Kalai lifted her right hand in a victory sign.

There were claps, mildly enthusiastic, but nothing like the sound of rolling thunderclouds that punctuated the end of PKB's speeches. The fishermen still stood, gleaming teeth and eyes. The women did not clap; they were much too demure. There was none of the dancing, rotating frenzy that a tiny part of her had wished for. A part of her had wished for the ability to hypnotise people and move them into acting stupidly. Kalai stepped back from the mike. She came away feeling like a newsreader having just read out the news. She had started the speech with a desultory 'Greetings'. She lacked sparkle, she lacked drama. She had been as exciting as day-old rice. She had been no better than those boring old Congress party politicians up north. The only difference was that her speech was short.

She sat down beside the big man, who avoided her eyes for the rest of the evening, as three long-winded speeches carried on, and the fisherfolk slept on their feet, only rousing themselves at intervals to contribute weak cheers over some verbal acrobatics or some witty piece of insult about the opposition party head, who used to be a writer of speeches before Kalai's time, and therefore accommodated himself to all kinds of witticisms. As the current speechmaker was saying, 'If the honourable ex-CM is making promises very similar to our own CM, then we must consider that these promises are as well worded as his speeches (he yawned, to some alert claps), and in that case, one can only conclude that his promises must also send people to sleep.'

In spite of these occasional contrived crowd-pleasers, there was an air of desolation that hung over them. It was as though all of them – Kalai, the fisherfolk, the politicians and the party cadre – were functioning as a body lacking its spirit. The spirit was PKB. She then knew she had absolutely no place in this business. She had neither the talent nor the interest to dabble in politics. After she dragged herself through to the end of the campaign, she would go back to her ladies' clubs, maybe even move to Bangalore, for a change of scene. This was not her cup of tea.

~

Maran left her back at her guest house and hurried away as if she carried the smallpox.

'To discuss strategy before the next public meeting,' he said, as a parting shot.

She knew that she had sorely let them down. She was as effective as a cardboard cut-out of PKB, and of that they had plenty. In spite of all her glamour and her star status, she could not make an impression on the diehard fans and base electorate in PKB's own constituency. She would only do worse in the others, where the voters were not as sympathetic. They might even boo her, or walk out.

How could she back out now? Could she claim a headache? But for the next four days? She walked from her bed to the bathroom and back. The silence around her pressed upon her skull. She really needed to talk. But there was no one. She could call somebody. She picked up the phone and dialled the numbers. When the phone began ringing, she realised her folly and cut off the line. Anju had a way of knocking the air out of her when she was down. But really, she had been calling Shekar. Dead Shekar. He would have listened without a sound. Then he would have told her she could do anything, she was that kind of a woman. He wouldn't have been lying, because he really did believe that. She would have felt so much better after that call. He was the only person who had been utterly on her side. Apart from PKB. But what did she really know about PKB? You couldn't separate the man from the myth.

There was a knock on the door and it opened as she turned away. She couldn't face anyone, anyone.

'Baby.'

Kalai turned around and burst into tears.

Ilango carefully closed the door so it stood open just an inch, then moved nearer. He hovered awkwardly while Kalai cried. He didn't say a word till she finished, dried her eyes, blew her nose with her handkerchief and said, 'Sit down, sit down.'

'All well?' he said.

Then, positioning herself on the sofa while he perched on a stool, she harangued him. 'How could you disappear for ten years and suddenly turn up like this? Did you not think at least a letter now and then would have been welcome, at least to let me and Anju know you were still alive? Do you know how many times I nearly went to the police, or hired men to look for you?'

Here she paused, with a stab of realisation that she had never actually done either. She had always thought about doing something, and nearly did, but never did, in fact.

'Baby,' he said, 'you did not have need of me.'

'And now you think I do?'

'Yes.'

'You are right.'

They both smiled. Ilango looked exactly as he had ten years ago. She knew she couldn't say the same for herself. She was plumper. She looked her age.

'You look exactly as you did twenty years ago,' he said to her.

'Enough. Were you at the meeting? Is that why you decided I need help?'

'Yes,' he said. 'You look unhappy. And there was nobody with you. No one of any account.'

'Shekar's gone.'

'What happened, baby?'

'Cancer. But it was quick. Three months from start to finish. And PKB . . . well, he looks poorly. He's gone to America for heart surgery. He told me throat, of course. Even to me, he would not admit how he really is.'

'How is mummy?'

'Like a grindstone. You know, she has always been . . .'

'Herself?'

'Yes. Do you know, just before you walked in, I was so distraught, I picked up the phone and nearly called her. Can you imagine? That was why I was crying when you appeared. With the shock at my own behaviour.'

Ilango laughed.

'So what have you been doing with yourself?' she asked him.

'After I last saw you, I nearly died from jaundice.'

'But I thought you were recovering.'

'It took me months to get out of my delirium. I hovered on the brink. My poor granny, the exhaustion of bringing me back to life sent her early to her own grave.'

'How old was she?'

'Sixty.'

'She had a full and good life then.'

'That is so. I finally got back to my own self, but then I find that everything is somehow changed within me.'

'What changed?'

'I did not want to come back to Madras. I read that you were settled and happy, and no longer in the movie business. I thought I would stay for a while, and learn what this growing business is all about.'

'You got into farming?'

'And after ten years of it, I still do not know the difference between a peanut and a groundnut.'

'Why did you come?'

'This morning I wake up and a couple of the village good-for-nothings are hovering at the doorway, excited like rootling pigs. "What is it?" I ask them. And they have the cheek to tell me, there is a rumour that your Kalai madam is appearing in a political meeting, to campaign with PKB, and they are going to do a whole movie song and dance on the stage, hold hands and sing about the PFD. And did I know anything about it, you know, being old friends and all. And they snigger like pigs put to bleed.'

'Ah?'

'That simply made my blood boil, you can imagine. That was it. I told my brother-in-law, "Here, you are doing a much better job of growing and cutting anyway." I arrived in time for you to start cranking up the microphone.'

Ilango grinned, and Kalai noticed with horror his teeth were brown.

'You take paan now?'

'Yes, but if you don't like it . . .'

'I don't like it.'

'Then I chew paan no more.'

'What did you think of my speech?'

'Baby, why do you want to know what I think?'

'There is no one else to tell me.'

He shifted on the stool, nodded to himself, as if gathering his thoughts.

'Baby, I will tell you what I think, in the language I understand. You know we say masala movie? Something for the whole family. Comedy for the children, action for the men, sentiment for the women. You see, the last few years, these city-bred blighters are making these so-called art films. People sit and cry all the time, bad things happen to them at the beginning, and worse things happen at the end. Their lives never get any better. They never wear any nice clothes or go to Switzerland to sing and dance in their dreams. In short, they behave very unlike real people.'

'You mean *like*?' Kalai laughed.

Ilango ignored her interruption. 'So nobody watches these new films. Everyone still goes and sees PKB and Balamani movies. Now I'm not saying your speech was like the art movie, nothing bad like that, baby, but it was not like a good masala movie. You must speak to the hearts of the people. You must entertain, make them laugh, make them weep. Make heroes and villains. Your talk of intellectual blah-blah is only good in your convent school, baby.'

'Is it now?'

Ilango laughed, and Kalai winced at the sight of his teeth.

'You really must go to a dentist,' she told him.

'What's that?'

She sighed at his obstinacy. Smiled as well.

'Fine. I am tired. I must get up early tomorrow morning to leave for Madurai.'

'I will be at the door at five, baby.'

'We will practise my next speech on the way.'

~

The next morning, she came out of the guest house, expecting Ilango to have stashed her luggage in the car boot and be waiting by the open back door. Instead, he was having a shouting match with the big man.

'What's going on?' she asked them.

'He cannot come with us,' said Maran. 'There is no room.'

'He will sit with me, in the back. Your seat in the front is safe.'

'Who is he, anyway? For all I know, he could be a JFD spy.'

'He is with me and that is enough.' Kalai struggled to control her anger. There was no point in creating an enemy when this could be resolved with all sides at peace. She would be diplomatic. She said, 'But since you are the man in charge, I will tell you who he is. He is my PA. He is going to help me with my speeches on this trip.'

'PA?' The big man looked Ilango up and down. She saw what Maran saw. A thin man in a frayed shirt and a filthy, cheap veshti. All she had seen last night was his face. She had not realised he looked like an impoverished bumpkin, straight from a PKB movie. But then she felt anger that Maran should dictate terms as to who could or couldn't sit beside her. She would be polite, defer to him, and still have her way. After all, he was in charge of the whole campaign of hers. If he left, she wouldn't know whether to turn left or right.

Before she could say something conciliatory, he said, 'Some PA. Does PKB know about this?'

That was it. Kalai snapped, 'He is coming with me. He is my PA. If you don't like it, you can come in another car and call up PKB to whine about it. Don't stand here complaining now. I have work to do.'

She got into the car. Ilango got in through the other door. She could see the driver's indecision as he sat there, hands on the steering wheel. She stared at his face in the rear-view mirror, willing him to obey her. He darted a nervous glance at the mirror, then started the car. A few moments later, while the driver pretended to dust the dashboard and say prayers to the little goddesses lined up there, Maran opened the front passenger door and got in without a word.

'Good man,' said Kalai. She hoped she would never see him again after the campaign.

In spite of the big man's brooding back obscuring their sky like a rain cloud, Kalai felt free and light-hearted for the first time since Shekar's death, and in spite of the circumstances.

'The problem at Karaikudi,' Ilango said to her, 'is that you weren't speaking directly to the people, in a language they understood.'

'I don't know any fisherfolk language,' said Kalai. They hadn't moved five hundred yards, and already he was sticking it in.

'No, baby,' said Ilango, and Kalai saw Maran's neck twitch. 'It is just that you were talking to them like a newsreader. It is better to talk like you are there in person, you know, face-to-face, like you are a well-wisher and a neighbour, as if you are superior to them, and not one of their own.'

'How can I be superior as well as equal to them?'

'Cinema, baby. Talk cinema.'

'How?' She heard the desperation in her own voice.

'OK, you are going to Madurai. What do you know of Madurai and its people?'

'Nothing. I have never been there before.'

'Never mind.'

'There is that big temple there, but we are an atheist party.'

'No, no. Temples divide people. What you do know, I will tell you, PKB was the king of Madurai in nineteen fifty-five, in *Maduraiyai Meeta Sundarapandyan*. In the movie, he played the Pandya king, the greatest king of Madurai, who saved the city from many a defeat, did good to the people. The film ran for a hundred days. So you say, "Who you want to vote for, you people? Some no-good dialogue writer from Madras, or your own Sundarapandyan to rule you justly and wisely?" People will catch what you talking about immediately. They will laugh and feel clever.'

Kalai said with mock seriousness, 'You think I should talk like that? Who you want to vote for, you people?'

But Ilango didn't read her humour. 'No, no,' he said, 'put it in good Tamil. Your style of talking, baby.'

'OK, what else?'

'You could insult the opposition more forcefully.'

'Use movie dialogue style of insulting?'

'They might think they are mighty as mountains . . .'

'. . . but we are the flood that will wash them away.'

~

The meeting grounds at Madurai were even bigger than in Karaikudi. A restless crowd had gathered, large and urban, and though most of them were dyed cotton PFD supporters, there were also pockets at the back who jeered and made hyena calls as the speeches carried on. Kalai was scheduled to speak last. She felt sure this was Maran's revenge for the previous morning's fracas. Ilango, in the melee of minions at the back of the stage, whispered encouragements to her, but she hardly heard him. It was noisy everywhere. The crowds chattered among themselves, the minions chattered to the speechmakers, and the speechmakers no one heard. One after another, they droned on in a tiresome manner. Like the people of Karaikudi, the people of Madurai had not been informed PKB wasn't coming. They stood there in disappointment, without the wit to realise they could leave. They were here, and they would stay till the end. She hoped they would. Or it would look like her presence triggered the emptying of the grounds. As though she was putting people off voting for PKB.

For the moment, the crowds stayed, and the speechmakers did their best to alienate a generous audience.

Finally, Kalai's turn came. The audience stood quieter than before, the whistles and cheers fading. A woman in an orange sari smiled at her from the front row. Kalai was, after all, the legendary actress. They hadn't seen her speak in person before. A rapt young schoolboy in a corner, waiting. Their minds were open. She must not give doubt a chance to enter into her head. She cleared her throat. The mike man adjusted the height of the microphone. She began to speak even as his fingers left the microphone stem.

'People of Madurai. Madurai. Where the Tamil of Sangam lives. Madurai. The heart of the Tamils. Madurai. Our oldest and grandest city. People of Madurai, you who are the blood of our blood, in two weeks' time you not only determine the fate of your own city in the coming elections, you determine the fate of all the Tamil people.' She paused for breath. The sound of her voice ricocheted in her ears.

'It is a bad time in the world. Poverty, corruption, the decline of morals. These are enemies within as well as all around us that we fight. No. We battle! We are in a war. And your king, the bravest and most noble king of Madurai, Sudarapandyan, "Maduraiyai meeta Sundarapandyan" himself is preparing for war. He is asking you, loyal citizens, brave souls, to join the fight. Take up the mantle and the sword, look around at your possessions, your rivers and fields. Look at your families. Fly. Fly to defend them from the evils of corruption, poverty and the hundred other enemies that besiege us. Fight beside your king, shoulder to shoulder. Our king who is determined to save you and all the Tamil lands from the outsiders, the Cheras, the Mughals, the British, and all the evils that they bring.'

She paused for effect, carried on before they could applaud or jeer: 'But you are saying, we are not in a movie! We are not in the costumes of the soldiers of the Pandya king. We do not have to fight the Cheras and the Mughals any more. The British left. The times may have changed, but the enemies remain, undefeated, in different forms, fooling you into believing you are safe. No, become alert and vigilant. Use your power. You may no longer need swords and shields. Then how do I fight? You ask. You have the power of the vote. Vote to keep your lands and wealth in good order. Vote to eradicate poverty and corruption. Vote for the only leader who has the interest of the common people at his heart, not the interests of his nephews, cousins, sons and daughters in the party hierarchy. Vote for the party of your King Sundarapandyan, who rises to battle every day on your behalf. Vote for PKB. Vote for the Coconut Frond!'

As she raised her fingers above her head in a sign of victory, flushed, she wondered if she had gone too far. She was only just becoming truly aware of the vast physical presence of the crowds before her. She had not watched their reactions at all through the speech.

The world seemed to hold on the in-breath. Her fate, her life itself seemed to hang, precarious, above some black chasm. Then the applause began. To her amazement, it rolled higher, bigger, like thunderclouds in the sky, till it became deafening. She wanted to stoop beneath its power. Instead, she stood taller, raised her hand with its victory salute higher. The people, it seemed, loved hyperbole.

~

It was a cool, rain-soaked morning in September. Kalai was travelling in her new car. There was the smell of new earth in the air. Clean, newly turned, fresh, alive. The smell of victory, she thought.

Returning from the election campaign, she had felt restless. She needed to change things in her life. She had the urge to throw everything away and get new things. People, objects, everything. She couldn't very well chuck Anju and Pushpa and buy a new mother and servant. Ilango was, in effect, brand new, returned like a talisman to herald the new phase of her life. But that was not enough. She roamed the house, ignoring Shekar's things, still waiting to be sent to a charity. She decided to get rid of her Ambassador car and buy one of the new makes, a Maruti. But there was nothing wrong with the Ambassador, so why change it? The new Maruti looked like a car from the future, even if it was laughably small. It would be a struggle for Anju to fit into it, so fat had she become. Kalai just could not bear the Ambassador any more.

This decision shocked not only Anju and Pushpa. Even Ilango was taken aback. When the car was delivered, they crowded around it and stared. Even some people on the road stopped at a polite distance, jaws slack. For once, they did not have eyes for Kalai, standing right there in all her yesteryear film-star glory. The car was more interesting.

'It is very red, baby,' said Ilango. 'Did they not have a black or a white model?'

'The Ambassador was perfectly fine, wasn't it?' said Anju.

'It was fifteen years old, Anju,' said Kalai.

'It is so small,' sneered Pushpa. 'Like a matchbox.'

'It is not,' said Kalai. 'Why don't you climb into it and see?'

'Ah, not me.' Pushpa sprang a couple of feet back, scowling, insulted by the impropriety.

'Don't be presumptuous,' snarled Anju.

Kalai smiled to herself. She had wanted to rattle Anju by inviting the servant to sit in the car before she invited her. Not that Pushpa would ever dare sit in something so precious as a car, even if a hundred Kalais and Anjus compelled her.

'Let's go for a test drive,' Kalai said to Ilango.

Anju had been, despite her reserve, first in the car.

And now, this preposterous vanity purchase was taking her to see PKB again.

'Put some music on,' she told Ilango.

The Maruti suited her, as the Ambassador never did. When she was a child, the Ambassador had seemed very grand, owned by rich, loving families who bought their children ice cream. These were children who confidently addressed strangers – for all were beneath them. The Ambassador, she realised now, had all these years made her feel like an impostor. The beggar crowned king for a day. Every time she had to go somewhere, she wondered if her errand was worthy of such a car. But the Maruti did not come with all that baggage. It freed her. And Ilango drove it. The agreed relationship was that he was a servant too, if a more touchable one than Pushpa.

'Ilango,' she said, 'you must always drive me from now on.'

'Yes, baby.'

Driver, PA, friend, though she would never embarrass him by voicing the last.

'Traffic,' said Ilango, 'is much worse than I remember.'

They were on the Marina Beach Road. Ilango refused to take the car on the smaller roads. It will get scratched, he said. It will get touched. It will get looked at. He treated the car like a virgin bride. But even on Beach Road, the widest road in Madras, they were surrounded by the slow grunts of oxen, rickshawallas and horses. Ambassadors and Fiats, buses and trucks, trumpeting horns to scatter the lesser beasts from their path.

The latest Ilayaraja hit spilled out of the cassette player. Ilango had spent two days stroking it before Kalai thrust a cassette into his hand and ordered him to turn it on. Now, he wouldn't turn it off even when she pleaded a headache. The thought of a headache led to the other looming ailment.

'I wonder if PKB is really all better,' said Kalai.

'He will be, baby. I and Anju madam did a special puja for him on the day of his big operation.'

'So that is what you were up to. All hush-hush behind my back. Where did you go?'

'To the Pillayar temple in Triplicane. We didn't tell you because you would have poured scorn.'

'I would have.'

'But you see, he will be all better. These American doctors might be very good at putting people right, but who knows if our Pillayar guides their hand during the operation or not, without us to persuade him with our pujas?'

'You surprise me sometimes with your astuteness in all kinds of matters.'

'Make fun all you want, baby, but you will know it is the Pillayar's work when you see PKB miraculously looking fifty years younger, romancing heroines like he used to.'

Kalai was comforted, though she would never admit it, to know that all the possible applications had been made to restore PKB to health.

The yellow walls of PKB's Adyar bungalow came into view. The last time Kalai had been there, at least fifty people milled about at the big iron gates and inside. His wife did not live there. His household consisted of all kinds, a mismatch of relatives, assistants and gofers. PKB's old assistant, Murali, curly-haired, chubby, opened the gates.

Getting out of the car, Ilango said, 'Murali! You are back too.'

'Ilango,' said Murali. 'Never in my dreams did I imagine you would pop out of one of these Maruti cars one day. You have gone up in the world.'

'How is Mr PKB?' asked Kalai. The sight of such emptiness around the building made her nervous.

'He is inside, expecting you. Go in, madam. He will tell you himself.'

'So he can talk?'

'Yes.'

There was something else. Murali looked uncomfortable. 'He is weak, but he can talk. He really wants to see you.'

Ilango waited outside. Kalai went in with Murali.

'You came back, I see,' said Kalai.

'He'd rather have me around than anyone else.'

'Where are all the people that are usually here?'

'I sent them all away. He didn't want to be disturbed.'

'That is not like PKB. He still has to run the state, doesn't he?'

Murali opened the door to PKB's study and said, 'I will be here when you come back out, Kalai madam.'

She continued to stand, holding the door, after Murali left. There was something ominous about the atmosphere at the Adyar bungalow. Where were his family? Where was his wife? Were they inside, standing around his bed, like they did when . . .? Without finishing that thought, she thrust herself through the door.

'Arasi, you have come.' She was relieved to hear PKB's voice, sounding weak, but clear.

She approached the divan where he lay, propped by cushions, exactly as she had left him the last time she had seen him. He did not wear his woolly hat and sunglasses. His eyes were sunken into his pallid face. His bones showed through, like a skull. A smell came off him, of tinctures and ointments, used no doubt to arrest, or attempt to arrest, the decay underneath, but which still wafted insidiously up.

'You are well?' she asked him.

'As well as I'll ever be.' His voice sounded as though his diaphragm had been sandpapered away.

'Congratulations, Chief Minister,' she said, clutching the hands he held out to her. They felt like paper gone soft.

'All thanks to you, Arasi. They told me of your clever speeches. Did Ilango help?'

'A little bit, yes.' She smiled to take the lie out of the 'little bit'.

'And I won the election, just like that, lying unconscious in some godforsaken mausoleum of a hospital.'

'Godforsaken? I thought you were an atheist.'

'God makes a lot of expressions powerful. There must be a god, at least for the sake of conversation.'

'So who is going to run the state while you are getting better?' Her cheeks flushed hot. He was not going to get better.

'This body is a broken shell. If only I could transfer my mind into a twenty-year-old body. That new boy, for example, Kamalahassan. He would do. But to answer your question, my dear, the state will have to run itself for a while. Why else have I appointed so many ministers and civil servants? Not to mention all the pen- and paper-pushers in the public services?'

'When did they do a good day's work without your whip at their backsides?' said Kalai, but her mouth was talking while her heart sank. First Shekar. Now PKB.

'Never mind that. Let us talk about you. You did no more than I expected, you know.'

'You should have seen the first speech. It was terrible.'

'But the second! Madurai meeta Sundarapandyan. You know what they are calling you now, don't you?'

'No.'

'Some quarters of Madurai are whispering that you are indeed Meenakshi.'

'The goddess?'

'Meenakshi who came to war by the side of her mortal husband, Sundarapandyan. Who defeated his enemies, crowned him king of Madurai, ruled with him for three thousand years.'

Kalai laughed. 'Is this your way of appointing me successor,' she joked. 'To ensure three thousand years of PKB legacy?'

PKB opened his mouth, but no words came. A light seemed to go out in the room. Kalai realised what her words had implied. She had just told him to his face that his time was come, that he should be thinking of a successor. No doubt he already had one in mind. Some young minister he was secretly grooming, or even openly. She would know if she followed politics. Some cousin. Some brother-in-law. That was the usual way. Maybe he had some illegitimate son stowed away. A pale shadow of his father, but with enough physical resemblance to convince the Tamilians that he could take on his mantle. And here she was, teasing him about his plans.

'Arasi,' he said, 'I have no successor.'

'Oh.' She assumed a false brightness. 'Successors have a way of appointing themselves.'

'I don't believe in successors.' With sudden energy, he raised his head an inch from the cushion. 'I made the party what it is. I built it up, brick by brick. Not to hand it over to some thug, so he and his friends can run around chewing up everything like rats. There isn't a single person I trust,' he rasped.

'Even me?' She sounded plaintive to herself. His words hurt far more than she could have believed they would.

'I trust you with my life, my queen. But we are not talking about my life. We are talking about the future of the Tamil nation. If you were a man, with interest in politics, if you had spent time running a ministry, I might consider you, just for a minute, no more.'

The effort of his speech made him wheeze. He lay back, closed his eyes.

Kalai felt a prickling of irritation.

'As the matter stands,' continued PKB, eyes still closed, 'nothing doing.'

She was about to turn away, but she surprised herself saying, 'You yourself jumped into politics at the highest level without any experience.'

But he did not seem to hear. His eyes opened, wandered to the ceiling and there was a smile, a ghoulish, cunning smile, on his face. 'They all ask me. Who? Who, after you, PKB? You know what I say?'

'No.'

'You know what I say? I don't care. They can all fight it out among themselves. Like the other man said. What was that he said?'

'Which man?'

'After me, the deluge.'

~

It was Pushpa's habit to turn on the radio first thing every morning. The day Kalai didn't wake up to a film song blaring into her room like sunlight through the window, she knew, even as she drifted, still half asleep, that something was wrong. The radio silence was broken by a newsreader announcing the CM's demise. Fighting the feeling of numbness that stole over her limbs, Kalai sat up, and began to go through the motions of getting dressed. She could not decide between a black sari and a dark green sari. Black, after all, was the political colour of all the Dravidians. She chose green and began to think about what she ought to do. She should go to his house, and sit by his head. It was then the bludgeon of grief struck her, and she had to lie down again.

~

'We must go,' said Anju. 'We knew him so well. It will be disrespectful.'

'We do not know the situation, Anju,' said Kalai, dropping the phone receiver on the cradle. Her forefinger ached from dialling. She had been calling all of PKB's numbers, his secretary's, even his family's, for several hours, but they were all engaged. After forcing herself out of bed, she had found it distracting to plan the practical matter of going to the funeral house, but she hadn't imagined it would be so difficult.

When Anju and Ilango had gathered with her in the morning to decide what to do, Ilango had said, 'You cannot just turn up at the house. We have to study the lay of the land first.'

'What do you mean by that, Ilango?' she had exclaimed. 'Whatever our on- and off-screen relationship was, that was donkey's years ago. I just publicly campaigned for him all over the state. What are they afraid of? That I would claim ownership of his body like some cheap mistress?'

'It is not about the past, baby. It is about the future. In politics, baby, one has to be careful with one's moves. We must get the timing right.'

'What timing?'

'Whether to turn up at the house where the family is, where there is a long queue to view him, whether to join the procession, or go straight to the beach, where they will stop for the leaders to garland him.'

Her head spun. 'OK, you go then, find out what you can from Murali.'

Kalai couldn't fathom why it was so complicated. Really, she ought to simply go to the house with a garland, commiserate with the family, sit for a while, like at any funeral. Even hug and cry with whoever wanted to hug and cry with her, if she felt so moved. Presumably, there were thousands of people waiting to throng the procession. All would attempt to get within touching distance of the body. She wasn't a political leader, so she couldn't really turn up at Marina beach and garland his body in front of the photographers and press. She should go to the house. Simple. Why was Ilango complicating things? What did the family care now if his screen wife of ten years, even if his 'one and only queen', turned up to pay her respects, when he was a shell of a body waiting to be cremated? She had long ago lost her charms and her man-grabbing abilities. She was halfway to the grave herself. Middle-aged.

'Get me a glass of lime juice, Pushpa.'

There was no answer. Pushpa wasn't hovering at the doorway of the kitchen or in a corner of the room, as she always did. Kalai called out again, but there was no answer. She waited a few minutes and called again. Anju, immersed in her thoughts at the other end of the sofa, roused herself to say, 'Where has that girl gone to?'

Was Anju cracking up too? To call her a girl. Pushpa was going on forty-six, at least. Perhaps Anju still imagined they were living in that small portion on Cubber's Road, and Pushpa had just been brought in with the first of Kalai's cheques. Pushpa then, a glowing girl in her twenties, still hoping to marry and flee this nest of waspish women. Well, marriage did not get you far. Look at her. Ten years of marriage, now back to square one. And there was no way to guarantee Pushpa would not have ended up with a drunk husband who beat her, as most of them did in her class of society. Pushpa then would have clung to the memory of her time in Anju and Kalai's house as golden glory days. That scenario was more probable than Pushpa ending up in a happy, cinema climax of the maidservant who got married to the comedian cook and remained content in poverty.

Forty years of marriage. Kalai's thoughts turned to PKB's wife. What was she feeling now? What could Kalai possibly say to comfort her?

A faint, rhythmic sound came from the kitchen. Kalai unbent her stiff legs, went into the kitchen. Pushpa was sobbing, her head resting against the mixie jar.

'What did Anju say now?'

She shook her head, unable to speak, still choked with sobs.

'What is it, Pushpa akka?'

Even the buttering of her name with the suffix of big sister did not raise Pushpa from her gloom. Kalai waited, without interrupting, till the sobs subsided, and Pushpa spoke.

'It is the CM.'

'You never even met him, Pushpa. The only time he visited us at home, we hadn't yet got you in the house.'

Pushpa's eyes flashed. 'How cruel of you to think it is all to do with you, baby. We all have feelings too, you know. Some of us have feelings for the people, all of the Tamil people. We all are heartbroken. He was our leader. He gave us hope, delivered on promises. Now there will be no one worth stepping in his shoes. It will all go to the dogs.'

'Pushpa!' Kalai could only laugh, although tears stung her eyes too. She was bewildered by Pushpa's sentiment. 'I did not know you were a PFD cardholder.'

'That is because you never paid any attention, baby. Go back to the sofa. I'll bring your lime juice.'

～

Ilango returned.

'You took your time,' said Kalai.

'I had to muscle past thousands of people,' he said, grabbing a jug of water and pouring it down his throat.

'You look like you've been fed through a rice mill.'

'And when I got near the house, nobody would let me in. There wasn't anyone I know. Nearly came to blows.'

'You would think at a time like this they would show respect,' said Anju.

'Ah, now PKB is gone, there is no one to control these vultures. They are all trying to grab a piece.'

'So did you see Murali?'

'Yes. It was difficult, but at last I got to him. He was cowering in a corner. PKB's family isn't making all the decisions. It is the political types, of course. The one who gets to make the most decisions, act most authoritative, gets the biggest piece of the pie.'

'What do we care about all that? Let us go.'

'Wait, baby. It will be hard for you to get to the house. There will be obstacles.'

'Everyone knows who I am. They will be expecting me. Even his family, I daresay.'

'The family is immaterial, baby. The problem is exactly that everyone is expecting you.'

What did Ilango mean? If everyone was expecting her, how could she not go?

'I've heard enough of your nonsense,' she said at last. 'I'm going. Come, Anju.'

'Wait. Murali said, on no account bring Kalai's mummy. Things will get ugly. They will stoop to anything.'

Anju blanched. She had been getting up, but now she

sank back into sofa. 'I don't know what is going on,' she said. 'What have I done?'

'Nothing, Anju,' snapped Kalai. She said to Ilango, 'OK, let us go then, you and I.'

'Murali said they are going to take the body out soon.'

'Well, then let us hurry. I don't want to go on the silly procession. We must catch them before they take the body out.'

~

About a mile from PKB's house, the crowds came into view, thick as bees. Ilango slowed down. Kalai pulled her sari over her head, and wished she had brought two more men with her, perhaps the gardener, and the mechanic down the road who was a strong man. Ilango was not the type to part the crowds with his presence.

'Don't slow down,' said Kalai, her voice sounding strained to her own ears. 'Keep your hand on the horn.' Crowds made her claustrophobic. All these thousands of people who knew her, studied every millimetre of her features in photos and film, recognised her voice in their sleep, while she knew nothing of them.

Horn blaring, the engine in first gear roaring like a beast, the red Maruti squeezed through the reluctantly parting crowd. There were cries and songs of lament, singly and in groups, coming from the people. The people made space for the car as well as they could. They reached the front gates.

As they got out, the crowd elbowed in for a closer look.

Panic gripped her. She pushed her sunglasses up her nose and her sari firmly over her forehead. Still they knew her.

The ghost of her name circled around in whispers. Kalai had never felt so oppressed in her life. They moved towards the gates, Ilango carrying a six-foot-long rose garland.

Big, burly, ex-convict political meat stood inside the gates, right up against it. They wore PFD colours.

Kalai waited for the gates to open. She was surprised that they didn't recognise her and jump to open them. They didn't even meet her eyes. Were they from another state? It couldn't be.

Then the gates opened a crack and a thin man, studious-looking, with a pot belly and a long-suffering air, slipped out.

'Open the gates,' she told him.

'I'm very sorry, Kalai madam,' he said. 'We are taking the body out now. There is no time.'

'You can wait for one minute while I pay my respects,' she said. 'And who are you, anyway? Part of the family?'

'Our leader's political party was his dearest family. We are all like his sons.'

'I'm sure,' she snapped, 'like Dridarashtra's sons. Hundred demons from one ball of flesh. Open the gate.'

'The family also, his real family, has sent word that you are not to be allowed in.'

She had thought Ilango a fool for being paranoid. She had been naive. With so many people watching, they were locking her out as if she were some beggarwoman gatecrashing a wedding feast.

'I'm not talking to you,' she said. 'Go and send someone in charge.'

'I'm the only one who will speak with you,' said the squirrel man.

'Send PKB's brother or cousin or someone. He has a brother-in-law, doesn't he? Jaivel. Go and send him to me.'

He just stood there. There was a commotion at the entrance of the house. And the women inside set up a high and mighty wail. PKB's body emerged. Kalai felt herself go rigid. Grief swayed her. She had forgotten, in the last few minutes, that PKB was actually dead. A part of her had been noting the squirrel man's behaviour to complain to PKB later. But, of course, there was no PKB. Only his self-appointed 'sons' of the party. Only anarchy. So that was what he meant by 'the deluge'.

The gates opened. An open truck backed into the compound, its flat bed transformed into a flower draped boat. They laid a woven green coconut mat in the middle, and then brought PKB's body to lay across it. He wore his woolly hat and sunglasses. He seemed more an effigy of himself. She couldn't see from such distance if he was wearing his watch or ring, if his lips were coloured rouge.

Women milled around the body, beating their chests, tearing their hair. Servants and relatives. A few funeral junkies, no doubt. Where was his wife? There, supported by two women, weeping in her wedding sari, hair full of jasmine flowers, forehead loaded with vermilion. After the body left for the cremation ground, in a separate ceremony, they would break the bangles on her wrist, strike the vermilion from her forehead, empty her hair of the jasmine. They would garb her in a white sari. A gruesome custom. All these years his wife had been reluctant to emerge from PKB's shadow. Now that PKB wasn't there, would there still be a shadow to hide in, or would she have to expose herself?

Kalai could not get near PKB's body even now with the gates open. A sea of goons stood around the truck, and some had an especial eye on her.

A hush fell over the people outside the gates. She was at the tip of this vast spear of gaping grief, and yet was not allowed beyond the gates. Her eyes sought PKB's wife again. She couldn't remember her name, for a moment. Then it came to her. Kamala. She could see her face. She had always been rather unremarkable in Kalai's eyes. There was no drama in her countenance. But now, grief had softened her eyes, her age had leeched the flesh from her facial bones. Kalai saw her as though upon the screen. A tragic queen of Tamil cinema.

As Kalai studied her face, Kamala looked up and met her eyes at last, and the man she was with turned too. It was the squirrel man who had blocked her path into the house. Kamala turned swiftly away. Maybe she was simply turning towards another man addressing her. Maran. He seemed energetic. He was angry. He was shaking his hands and head. Was this about her too? She could not remember so many people talking about her, obsessing about her like she was some malevolent creature. What had she done?

Maran strode towards Kalai, people scattering in his

wake, an expression of someone about to fell a tree. Kalai took a step back, clutched Ilango's arm.

'You think you can usurp what is rightly ours by turning up here?' Maran's voice boomed over them. The crowd, that great spear of grief, fell silent.

'And who are you to have the right?' said Kalai. Her voice sounded calm, even though her fingernails were tasting Ilango's flesh.

Maran declaimed as if he was in a theatre play. 'Who I am? Ask yourself who you are. What pedigree do you have? How dare you turn up to sully this holy temple where lies the body of our leader? How dare you think you can simply take over his mantle, you, who are merely his actress?'

Kalai had not expected this. She raised a chin towards Kamala, and said, 'You think I want to replace Mr PKB, or his wife?'

Someone in the crowd laughed. From far back. So they could all hear her.

'Do not utter his name with your mouth. You sully it. Now leave before we chase you away.'

Kalai found herself pushing past Maran. She was both incredulous and furious. Too angry to be cautious. When she reached Kamala, a ring of goons blocked her way. But Kamala could hear her. So Kalai spoke.

'What is the matter with all of you? I have simply come to pay my respects.'

Kamala gazed at Kalai without speaking. Kalai saw how exhausted she looked. There was a vacancy in her dilated pupils. Kamala, poor bereaved Kamala, was bereft of reason.

At last the widow spoke, her voice a papery whisper that nonetheless carried right through the crowd. 'What do you know about respect, you whore?'

~

Above the throbbing in Kalai's head, faint sounds of chanting reached her. 'Long live Kalai Arasi!' Another section of the crowd began, feebly at first, then strongly as more voices joined in, 'Long live Kamala-ma!'

Somehow, Kalai was outside the gates again. Ilango was urging her to go home. They had done all they could.

Amid a crescendo of ululations and drums, the truck moved out, and started the snail-pace procession. Kamala was in one of the chairs near PKB's head. Maran and his goons sat or stood around PKB's body. White and PFD colour-clad politicos surged from the house and grounds like locusts, and followed the truck.

'They can't chase me away like this,' said Kalai. 'If I can't pay my respects like friends and family, then I will walk with the crowds all the way to the beach.'

'In the crowd?' said Ilango. Amid all these thousands, this heaving ocean of people, she was alone with Ilango.

'Yes,' she said. 'Yes.'

Ilango sighed, pointed to the house. 'Have you noticed the press standing huddled in that corner? They have long-lens cameras.'

'I am not doing it for the press,' she said.

~

They walked. The people surged around. PKB's truck was a smudge of colour in the distance, a beacon the people followed. And she was one of them. Only one among many. She tried not to think about how many there were. How many were trying to get close to her, to touch her. It was a mistake. She should have gone home. At the pace they were crawling, it would take them half a day to get to the beach. It would be after sunset. And she would be eroded, her skin stripped away by the brushing, touching crowd. She felt a little faint. But she could not faint. She must not.

'Baby . . .'

Ilango supported her back. She closed her eyes, tried to shut out the sighs, calls, wails, anger, the stink of sweat, the overwhelming humanity. If she could think of a comforting thought, she might revive. Cocooned by Shekar's arms, her head on his chest. She fought her way out of the grasping hands of the crowd and ran to Shekar. He was freshly showered, pristine, clad in crisp white. He held her. But that was a fantasy. He was dead. He could not help her. He was dead, and so was PKB. She had to support herself.

She opened her eyes again. She wasn't dizzy any more. She took a deep, steadying breath. She could not shut out the reality of the situation she was in. Foolishly, she had chosen to challenge these monstrous politicians, most of whom she had never even heard of before, with this self-sacrificing penance-pilgrimage. Walking like the commoners, with the commoners. Now she was scared stiff, paralysed by claustrophobia. Yet she had to face them.

She had to come to terms with it if she were to finish the procession with her sanity intact.

For the first time, she looked properly at the people around her. Many were women, some quite old, but sinewy as hardened tree branches. And men. But they were just men, not monsters. Farmers and workers. Bus and auto drivers. Masons. Plumbers. Ilango. Murali.

Murali too was beside her.

'You did a very good thing, Kalai madam,' he said. 'I'm so pleased you have decided to take it on.'

'Take it on?'

'The fight.'

They walked on, very slowly.

An old lady, walking more briskly than Kalai, poked a man's foot out of her way with her stick. The man yelped, streamed abuse, but she acted deaf.

'Walk with me, grandma,' Kalai called out.

The old lady smiled a toothless smile. She would have been a perfect cast for any of PKB's movies. He was always hugging an old, toothless crone while singing a public service message.

People made way for the old woman to walk with Kalai.

'Child,' said the woman, slurring her words, 'you are the only one, among all these vultures, who can sustain our leader's great vision.'

A kind of energy flowed into her. She felt revived as though she had just poured a cool draught of water down her throat.

'You are the only one fit to lead,' said the old lady.

Someone shouted, 'Make way for madam to get closer to the truck.'

The people shuffled this way and that, allowing Kalai, with Ilango and Murali, to get closer. A number of PFD party members – 'Even a junior MLA or two,' whispered Ilango into her ear – scuttled like ants over a mound of sand, joined her, spread out to flank her like a general's guard.

Then she was beside the truck. The goons in the truck watched, muttered among themselves, as Kalai put a proprietary hand on the side of the truck. She felt the soft, wilting flowers under her hand, the throbbing of the truck's engine beneath. Through the layers of metal, wood and coconut leaves, she imagined touching PKB's body. She wondered if the people saw that she was channelling his spirit into herself. She hoped they did. It was, what? It was . . . power.

The goons and PKB's wife could only look on uselessly as Kalai became an integral part of the procession. They could not dare touch her now. Hundreds of people, including common PFD cadres, surrounded her and the truck. They chanted, 'Long live Kalai Arasi. Long live PKB.'

She strode like a queen to lay her dead king to rest.

2005

Tulasi uncoiled the black wires carefully, wound them around the table legs, before plugging them into the sockets. Then he did a mike test. 'Allo allo, mike test one two three.' The great hall hushed. A ringing sound, then a long whine came from the microphone. The press men and women glanced towards him, then beyond to the green room door, but no one of import had emerged. Tulasi was only the sound tech. The hall buzzed once more. A hive of bees.

The press conference's ultra secret location had been disclosed to them only half an hour ago. Tulasi felt fatherly towards them, these excited children. The hall bristled with pens, notepads, cameras. Phones rang, pressmen shouted, 'Allo allo,' and darted to the exits for a better signal. Tulasi's own Nokia, heavy as a brick, nestled in his shirt pocket. Out of a sense of professionalism, he hadn't called anyone about this momentous happening.

A man approached. 'Excuse me, is there anyone to regulate the questions?'

'Huh?'

'Where are Sathya's people? We need someone to give out tokens.'

Tulasi drew himself up. 'I am one of the superstar's people,' he said. 'I bear him here.' He pointed to his chest.

The man snorted and went away. Tulasi tapped the mike again, to underline his sentiment. All the local media was present, he noted, represented by one, if not two teams. Some carried logos in Kannada, Telugu, Malayalam and other languages he didn't recognise. The national media he recognised. NDTV, Tehelka. The door opened and a woman carrying an old, heavy camera stumbled in, followed by a man with a notepad. DD, said the logo on the camera. Late as usual. There, right at the front, given pride of place, were the BBC. Next to them some people from the Japanese media. The superstar had a huge fan base in Japan, in spite of his distinctly South Indian appeal.

Nearing sixty, insanely famous, he had never ever shifted his position of neutrality in all matters public. Philanthropy, yes. Politics, no. Now all that was about to change.

Tulasi surveyed the great hall, pretending he was still adjusting the mike. They said all Sathya had to do was give a slight nod of his head, and he could become chief minister within a day. As beloved as he was, it was impossible to read the man's mind. All that power at his fingertips, and he didn't grasp it. Like Caesar, he was offered the crown one, two, three times. He had refused so far.

Word floated around that he would stand as an independent candidate, win a seat, amass enough MLAs to take over the Secretariat on Beach Road. Goodbye to Kalai Arasi. But some contrarians said that even Superstar Sathya could not do it on his own. He would go with the Speechwriter against Kalai Arasi. But Tulasi did not believe that. Aligning with the Speechwriter would rub against the grain of his neutrality, his spirituality. It would be corrupting to his pure, moral, streaming, free-flowing self. Some New Delhi pundits let it be known that all his prestige rested on the fact that he was neutral, that the moment he picked sides he would lose his credibility, become just another politician hungry for power. Some diehard fans, desperate for the whole world to celebrate the superstar, desperate for every man, woman and child of every colour to have Superstar on their tongues and minds and souls forever, said he must stand alone, a lone crusader, against corruption and ugliness in public life.

Tulasi's flesh flowered in goosebumps as he went to wait at the doors, ready in case he was needed. The microphone could whine again, the wire could snap, Sathya might need the mike adjusted to his height. Tulasi nearly swooned at the thought of Sathya's breath misting his knuckles as he aligned the microphone to his super-mouth.

Sathya would stand as an independent candidate and bring about a Dharma-rajyam, a new era of morality, which would change all their lives for the better. With one swipe of his hand, with one announcement, he would begin the end of all the corrupt politicians, from both parties, and sweep clean the slate for everything to start afresh. They waited, with these words and ideas floating about. Tulasi and the press waited for the hour to strike. They knew he was punctual, and looked towards the door, all of them, and the door opened and, with those glinting sunglasses of his, the Superstar strode in.

~

The house was empty. The moon in the sky nearly full, the time nearly seven o'clock, and nobody had even come in to ask what she wanted for dinner. Kalai sat. She had stood at the window earlier. Now she sat. There was nothing to do. There was so much to do. There was always so much to do. But what? Everything seemed to have slipped her mind, just as the people in her household had suddenly slipped away.

There was a knock on the door. At last, she thought.

Ilango came in. 'Madam,' he said. 'Where has everyone gone?'

'Selvi is at her house.'

'I meant the others,' he said. 'The campaign is gathering momentum. I thought they would be camping in the house night and day from now on.'

It was years since he had involved himself in her political affairs, or even mentioned them.

'Come,' said Kalai. 'Let us walk in the garden. For so long, I have wanted to. And now, there is time, at last.'

The moon was a milky glow, a clouded glass disc. She hadn't tasted the night air in a long time. The trees, she wished she knew what they were, and the flowering shrubs. A dog would have enjoyed such a big garden. But a dog would have been miserable in a house where strangers came and went, day in and day out.

Ilango snapped a small twig from an overhanging branch. He was hugging the edge of the path, far enough away from her. Was it her status, or her girth? He had remained, defying nature, a skinny man, with a half-starved look. She did not know what he did with the salary she paid him. His clothes were ancient, ragged. His sandals had once belonged to Shekar. She had given Ilango all of Shekar's footwear. Even in the moonlight, they looked new.

Then she suddenly knew why. He kept them, preserved, probably wrapped in newspaper in a metal box under the bed, took out one pair at a time, and wore them down, one pair at a time. So, twenty years after Shekar's death, Ilango still had a new pair of sandals. Kalai felt something move inside her. She wanted to sit down and weep. It had been years, also, since she had cried before Ilango. Years since she had cried at all.

'The Superstar,' said Ilango, 'spoke a lot of words.' He was still standing with the twig in his hand, beside the branch. It looked as if he wanted to maintain a safe distance from her.

Kalai forgot her need to cry. 'The Superstar doesn't bother me,' she said. 'Who is he? Why does he involve himself suddenly in politics?'

'He said he has been forced to declare an interest since things turned so bad. He felt concerned for the state of the Tamil people.'

'Don't quote him to me,' said Kalai. Her irritation with the Superstar grew. It had been growing all day. In spite of recognising her own petulance, because it was Ilango and she could tell him anything, because he had once called her Baby, she said, 'He was a nobody when *I* was a superstar.'

Ilango came closer. 'He is a powerful man now. And he is not a bad man. People listen to him.'

'I don't care,' said Kalai. 'I am remote from it all. I am like the Buddha.'

She pulled away from Ilango. She walked faster, continued talking, even though it made her breathless to walk quickly nowadays. 'He thinks he is some young hero come to save the people from the evil queen. Let us not forget he is at least a few months older than me. When I was a heroine, he was tearing out ticket stubs in Bangalore. When I was entering politics, he was playing villain roles. Now he thinks he can dictate who the people vote for just because they allow him to wear a wig and dance with sixteen-year-olds around trees. What pedigree does he have? What does he know of what the people need? How dare he support the Speechwriter in the coming elections, a man who, even in his eighties, greedily partitions the state among his endless sons and nephews? And why?' She turned to face Ilango, suddenly cold as ice, defeated. 'Why did the Superstar not come to me, talk to me privately in the first place? Give me his ideas for how to do good for the people. We could easily work together.'

She could not see his face. The moon had gone behind a cloud. But she saw his hands, thrown up in the air, parallel to his elbows. 'Nobody knows how to reach you, madam. You sit like the goddess within her sanctum sanctorum.

There is always a ring of priests around you.' He cleared his throat. 'Your friends,' he said, 'their families, are the head priests.'

'Do not talk nonsense,' said Kalai. 'I have always been perfectly straightforward in my dealings ... with everybody. First thing tomorrow, I'll approach the Superstar, make him take back his statement.'

'You will make him? How?'

'Oh, I don't know. Talk sense to him. If he doesn't see the light, I'll stop him from filming another movie for the rest of his life.'

'Madam!'

Why was Ilango so shocked?

'I was not serious, Ilango. Remember, you used to have a sense of humour?'

Ilango laughed feebly. But was she joking? She used to have a sense of humour too. Sathya, they said, had good comic timing. She had seen one or two of his films. The moon emerged again. Kalai turned on her heel.

She could issue him a threat. Or she needn't bother. Did it matter if she lost the election, if people turned against her on Sathya's say-so? What would she do? Charity work. Gardening.

She would not think of such things. She had had enough of the garden. Enough of the fresh air. She could not give herself over to speculation. The Superstar could do what he liked. She would not waste her precious time and energy trying to change his mind. She would ignore him completely. She would campaign as if he did not exist.

'Come,' she said to Ilango, who stood limp and listless as a puppet with its strings cut. 'Enough chit-chat. Let us go and eat.'

1995

It wouldn't, no matter how Selvi pulled, meet at the back.

'Shall I tug harder?' said Selvi, in that honey-melon voice that Kalai found so pleasing after a lifetime of Anju's gruff tones. Selvi could coax any state secrets from Kalai with that voice of hers.

Unfortunately, Kalai's body wasn't as pliable as her heart. Selvi pulled harder, with an intake of her breath just behind Kalai's left ear, but then expelled it in defeat. There was a faint whiff of molasses.

'Nothing doing,' said Selvi. 'We will just have to get another size.' She released the vest.

Kalai's lungs filled themselves with relief from the confinement. She assessed her appearance in the mirror, marvelling at how, millimetre by millimetre, her flesh had expanded unnoticed, sneaking like an enemy under radar. Now here she was, all out of proportion to the image of herself she had in her head.

Was it because she spent so much time with Selvi, who was, at the moment, fatly her kin and kith? Like a twin. Same girth, same height. But Selvi's hair curled, and her skin was darker. A dark double. Selvi had bought the mirror. It was something out of those ridiculously furnished houses in Hindi movies.

Selvi moved away. Did Kalai move in so cumbersome a manner as well?

When the police expert had asked her for her measurements, Kalai had refused to give them. In fact, she had been so outraged that she'd considered firing him on the spot. Then she'd realised she wasn't sworn in yet, and that she had no powers to dismiss police officials. Not yet. The man had asked her to pick a size from among three. Small, medium, large. She had picked medium. She had thought, these things are made for men. And look at them. With their jowls and paunches. Medium would probably fit her quite loosely, she had thought.

They only had two hours to go for the ceremony, and she was quite at a loss as to how to manage it. There was nothing to do but order a bigger vest.

'Find that police expert,' she told Selvi. 'Tell him to get me a large size within the next hour. We have to leave at nine, sharp.'

Selvi made the calls, then came and stood by her, thoughtful. Kalai was trying on the 'coat' one more time.

'It fits very well,' said Selvi, but her eyes were on Kalai's feet.

'What's on your mind?' said Kalai.

'Wouldn't it be OK, for just this first time, to go out without the vest? I mean, if it doesn't arrive by nine. It is only a short ceremony, after all. There won't be any appearing in public.'

'Absolutely not,' said Kalai.

She turned around to imprint her words into Selvi's head.

'From today, I will never step out of the house without the vest.'

Yes, today was the watershed day. From today, she would rule, and in her kingdom, fear was banished. Like Karna, she would wear her divine armour. And with her armour, she would be invincible. She would step out into battle every day and no arrow would pierce her. No grubby male hand would lay a finger on her.

There was the sound of somebody at her door. The panicked tones of the outsider, the smug tones of her assistant. She stepped away from the mirror. She would dismiss the police expert if he failed her, promote him if he delivered. He would be the subject of her first orders, one way or another, as chief minister.

~

Finally, with the large-size vest secure, only ten minutes late, Kalai emerged from the house, holding Selvi's hand. Like well-trained dogs, rows of PFD party men waited outside the front door, at heel. The new fellow, she couldn't remember his name, came running to usher her towards the cavalcade in her drive.

For a moment, she was confused. Which car? Three Bentleys stood with their doors open. In front, the police jeep's lights flashed. Behind the cars were other cars,

Ambassadors, Tata Sumos, then police motorbikes. All for me, she thought. And all these second- and third-rung party men, some MPs also, waiting. They would get into the cars she didn't pick and then show off later that they were the CM's preferred travelling companions. She walked to the middle Bentley, then saw the driver.

'Where is Ilango?'

'Who, madam?' said the man, with his hand covering his mouth respectfully.

'My driver, you idiot.'

They all stood around clucking like chickens. From somewhere, Ilango shuffled forward. He looked a little lost. Beaten. Although, how could that be? They had just won. He wore a brand new white safari suit and cap like a European chauffeur. She had to smile. She could tell it had been taken out of its packaging just that morning, yet was already crumpled, the ironed, starched fabric now soft in the sweat and heat. Ilango's propensity for shabbiness. Grease stains on his cuffs. It was only ten minutes past nine. The other new driver, who had by now come around the car and was standing next to Ilango, suffering, alarmed, looked as if he had been imported along with the car.

But her Ilango. His hair was turning white on top of his ears. He was skinnier than a bamboo pole. He swallowed as if his throat was dry, as if it hurt to swallow.

'You will drive my special guests,' she told the other driver. 'Other states, when they visit, and Selvi madam to go shopping. And you can drive me on the days Ilango is on leave. But he is my personal driver, you understand.'

'Of course, madam.'

Was she imagining it, or did he look relieved?

'Ilango?'

'Yes, Kalai madam,' he said, and got into the driver's seat.

~

They turned into the road. Ilango's hands trembled on the steering wheel. The car was too much for him. Too sleek, too foreign, too powerful, too luxurious. She didn't feel that way, but he did. Was she too much for him too? Over the years, he had kept pace with her. Was he now falling behind? He was driving terribly slowly, considering the roads had been emptied specially for them.

'Do you remember, Ilango, our first time driving to the assembly?'

'Yes, madam.'

'In the red Maruti.'

'Yes, madam.'

After PKB's funeral, it had taken nearly five years to build her support base. Murali and PKB's secretary Vijayan lit the way. PKB's widow stepped into his shoes as CM till a general election could be called. An MP resigned his post and there was a by-election. Kalai won in a landslide. While Kalai dashed around making her presence felt in the world of politics, Kamala, ill and bewildered, eroded the party's popularity. Maran, like a rat from a sinking ship, left Kamala's PFD and joined the Speechwriter's JFD. The Speechwriter won the general elections. Maran became a ruling party MLA. Kalai retained her seat with a bigger majority. Kamala hardly appeared in public life. Opposition leader in name only, she was fast diminishing into dotage. Kalai was now the uncontested successor of PKB. She created trouble for the Speechwriter when she could. When the budget was released, Ilango drove her to the assembly to give her first speech slamming it.

She had clutched her notes. It had been one of those scorching April days, the kind of days when dogs and old people keeled over and died. The kind of day they warned would drive you insane if you ventured out at midday. She regretted the second cup of coffee she'd had that morning. It churned inside her stomach. Ilango bumped the car over a speed breaker and she entered the grounds. As a line of sentries saluted her, an uncharacteristically whimsical thought flared within her – all the roads she had taken in her life led here.

Into the sea of hubbub she waded and took her seat. As the discussion began of money, where it went, what it was supposed to do, she had a dawning realisation of what it was that lay within her grasp. It was as though she were entering a trance. Or were the heat and noise getting to her? She could count all the women in there with one hand. Kamala nodded in a corner. Poor woman. All this was beyond her. All she probably wanted was to sit in her puja room and read the Ramayana. Was it the sight of Kamala nodding that caused the rush of hope and butterflies into Kalai's stomach, that gave her the heady, confusing idea to be brave, to provoke?

The shouting, meaningless speech of whoever had the floor ended. The Speaker, already looking exhausted, the session not even halfway through, opened the floor to the opposition. Someone made to stand up – a man rumoured to be most keen to expedite Kamala's exit. Kalai, unencumbered in those days by her girth, came to her feet lightly. 'This budget,' she began, 'doesn't add up.'

'You need maths tuition,' someone shouted, to some 'Hear, hears' and guffaws, but she ignored them and went on. 'The welfare element is incompatible with the wealth element.' With all the force of her convent education, she took the budget apart. Every word landed perfect as a pearl.

~

The car whined in the wrong gear.

'Ilango.'

'Kalai madam?'

'It has been a while since you called me baby. Is it because I've become old?'

'Oh no, madam.' He jumped in nervousness, the car a little bit erratic.

'Then why do you treat me like I'm some monster you fear? Am I not the Kalai you raised by your hand?'

'I didn't, madam. Your mother raised you.'

She sighed. It was cruel to tease him. 'I know. It was only a manner of speaking.'

'Selvi,' she said, 'do you think I'm now too old to be called Baby by Ilango?'

'Yes, you are,' said Selvi, smiling.

In the rear-view mirror, she saw a small smile crack the surface of the tension on Ilango's face.

The car picked up speed.

They passed Stella Maris College, the 'Plan B Arts College' if her medical ambition had not come to pass. That was in another life. What would she have achieved, anyway? Saved a few lives, earned a comfortable living, bought a car, stayed like an apple in the fridge. She already had three honorary doctorates.

Selvi was humming. She said, 'It is amazing, isn't it, how they clear the roads just like that? It is so pleasurable to drive on empty roads.'

It was like Selvi to take pleasure in small things. She was a child at heart. It did Kalai good to be with someone like her. She was already the old cynic, taking after Anju. Kalai had barely noticed the roads emptied especially for her. She hadn't even known the difference, so jaded was she by novelty. And she wasn't that old. She was only now approaching middle age. Yes, they said forty-five was the new thirty-five. Selvi was her age too. It was good to have a best friend of one's own age. It was good to have a friend, at last.

Selvi lowered her window. The air streamed through. Without the traffic noise, she could hear the crows and the occasional cuckoo in the occasional tree when the cars slowed down to negotiate turns. Just like that, Selvi had made her notice the birds.

It had been through Ilango that she met Selvi in the first

place. In those days, when she had first moved into the big house on Pinky's road (she still thought of it as Pinky's road, although she had learned since moving here that Pinky's family was long gone), her only relief from politics had been to rent videos to watch in the evenings. She would send Ilango to the lending library on the corner. At first, she had been quite happy watching the old Tamil movies that he liked to watch himself, she on the sofa, he on the stool in a corner, or on the floor. But soon she wanted to watch Hindi movies, English movies.

Ilango didn't know anything of Hindi or English. Like an old aunty, he was scandalised by the thought of English movies. They have filthy scenes, he said. She rebuked him for his simple-mindedness. She ordered him to fetch the movie she wanted. He would go, and he would never remember the title. He would come back with some wholly different movie. Once, it was a movie about aliens eating people's brains and bleeding bright green. Then she started writing down the names of the movies for him. He would come back sheepish, saying they didn't have that one, present her with a Tamil movie he thought she would enjoy very much, primly perch himself on a settee.

Finally she was so fed up, she went herself. Selvi ran the video shop. It was her husband's, but she ran it.

Selvi laughed when Kalai mentioned Ilango.

'He and I are from the same community,' she said. 'Neighbouring villages.'

'Yes, he mentioned that,' said Kalai. But she had imagined Selvi would be someone ... provincial. Someone like Ilango. Selvi oozed urban. She spoke Madras Tamil. English words peppered in. Not much to look at. But a wonderful, generous smile, sparkling eyes. She wasn't fazed talking to Kalai. She worked in a wealthy area. She was used to all sorts.

~

The massive, gold-leafed gates of the governor's residence on Cenotaph Road opened to allow her cavalcade through. They drove slowly along the immaculate drive. On either side stretched preposterous green lawns. They were in the middle of a drought. Mature trees towered in the rising morning. The governor's palace loomed, dwarfing even the trees. They stopped beneath the broad, pillared frontage of the massive, old colonial building. They stepped out on to red carpets smoothed over densely packed earth, flanked by turbaned guards who saluted and clicked heels.

These impressive buildings and the pomp and ceremony, it occurred to Kalai, were designed for a race of men who thought themselves rulers of the world. Men who liked to hold themselves erect, who wore trousers with piping. They were not meant for people like her, and her white-clad followers.

The governor, coming towards her, was a short, dark man from Kerala, from some farming family, and his wife, with that terrible yellow sari on her dark complexion, dumpy, almost her husband's twin. The thuggish MPs and MLAs swarmed around the Grecian columns.

Her sari swished on the carpet. The governor's wife's jewellery tinkled as she walked beside Kalai.

The governor and his wife made chit-chat. Polite conversation. All was subdued and proper, and the ceremonial hall had the hallowed hush of a church. They went to the stage and sat on throne-like chairs. She didn't know where Ilango and Selvi had gone. There were rows upon rows of guests powerful and influential enough to deserve a seat at such a ceremony. Some schoolchildren in one corner. Uniforms on their rigid little bodies. Deaf-mute? Blind? No, lame. There were the wheelchairs, ready to be brought out. Had it been her idea? It must have been.

Her nerve held for the oath. Her English she mumbled, showing the hesitation, the modesty, of the woman who doesn't think of her own prowess in the coloniser's tongue, displaying the domestic nature at her core. Inoffensive. She was getting good at being a politician. When it was time to take the oath in Tamil, she stressed every syllable. She took her time, looked into the camera. She acted as though she was in a movie. The applause had been muted for the English oath. For the Tamil, it boomed against the domed ceiling.

~

Ilango was chirpy on the way back. He offered his analysis of her delivery to Selvi.

'Perfect,' he said, eyes sparkling in the rear-view mirror. 'It made one want to cry out with patriotism.'

'Niece's son,' said Selvi, laughing. It was an expression peculiar to her community, and Ilango's. She slipped like that when she spoke to him, and he liked it. He liked her. Ilango laughed as well.

The day was hot. The birds hid in cool nests and leaves. It was midday. The ceremony had been short, thankfully. The giving of the wheelchairs didn't take as long as she had thought. They brought the disabled all at once to the corner of the stage. Shouldn't keep the new CM waiting. So there was no agonising pause after each name was called while he or she hobbled out on sticks to receive the life-changing gift. It would have been torture to watch each one hurrying, limping, grinning their heart out, struggling with more enthusiasm than skill up the long, red stairs. No. It was better to have them clumped onstage, quickly dealt with.

'Baby,' said Ilango, 'what a day this is for you.'

Baby. She didn't feel like a baby any more. She felt like a madam. Wasn't it hearing her called baby that changed Maran's attitude towards her for the worse? She could still remember his face. His cheeks, that pulse on the side of his forehead quickening, the muscles hardening at the sound of Ilango's name for her. A mere boohoo baby. A spoilt, rich girl. A pampered, touchable girl begging to be touched by men like him. Men who dealt in pounds of flesh.

Till that moment, she had been the cinema star, beloved of PKB, beyond Maran's reach, beyond even his dream's reach. But the moment he knew she was vulnerable to the devotion of one such as Ilango, that she held the affection of merely a low-caste, uneducated movie gofer, car driver, shabby nobody like Ilango, then she became like one of the servant women every master thought he could touch. Like those Englishmen on tea estates groping the tea pickers.

'Maybe it is better if you don't call me baby any more,' she said to Ilango.

He nodded. She could not see his eyes.

It had to be done. Any chink in the armour . . .

~

What had triggered it, that first day she ever entered the assembly? Was it her glowing Kashmiri skin that made the men lose their hold on sanity? Was she too insulting towards the Speechwriter, a man thirty years her senior, two times chief minister and patriarch with two households? Did she call him names? Did she question his morals? Or worse, did she sneer at him with her convent girl put-downs? Could they all see the crack in time beyond which lay the certainty of her reign, and feel compelled to squash her while she was still small enough, weak enough?

After her budget speech, first, voices were raised. Incredulous. Angry. Then there was the pause before the insults. It was as though there was a cue, for the switch between the movie scene and the porn cutaway. Whore. Actress whore. Dancer. Cabaret dancer. PKB's slut. How to handle a slut. We will show you. There was the pause, again. And then, in unison, as if they had exchanged information telepathically, three, or was it four of them, flew across the benches towards her.

Maran, her old enemy, reached her first. Maran, who had known her when she was green-gilled, was beside her when she made her first stumbling speech in Karaikudi, who had peeped into her bedroom, stood in her small house, selected the places for her to sleep, borne witness to her being addressed as baby and chided by a mere servant. His hand was the first one. The others merely followed.

By the time she emerged back into the sun, the street, where, somehow, as if he had known what was happening, Ilango waited with the car engine running, her hair was dishevelled, her eyes red and weeping, her blouse torn, her sari a wreath of snakes. No one dared get in with her. Her useless advisers. Useless party men.

~

Now, today, her first day as chief minister, her face in the car breeze felt cold.

'Ilango, get me the best of the men when we go back. Immediately. I need to discuss this business of Maran.'

Selvi stirred. 'Is it the same Maran who . . .?'

'Yes.'

'He got a roasting in the elections, didn't he?' said Ilango. 'He's not favoured any more by the Speechwriter. Outlived his use.'

'All the same,' said Kalai. 'He needs to be taught a lesson. An example must be set.'

Ilango nodded.

'Good idea,' said Selvi. 'If you do nothing, he will always

have the upper hand. Psychological,' she added in English, tapping her forehead. 'He will strut around and say, I was the man who laid a hand on the CM . . . And people will respect him for that.'

The idea of Maran strutting around infuriated Kalai further.

'I will crush him so completely he will never strut again,' she said.

She had meant the words comically, like a PKB pirate movie villain. But it sounded deadly serious to her own ears.

Ilango laughed a child's ugly laugh of glee.

'We will plan what to do with him,' said Selvi.

'I already know,' said Kalai.

A fleeting voice of disapproval in her head. Anju's voice. But Kalai no longer had to heed Anju's voice, real or imagined.

~

Old age had sucked Anju's poison and left her a prune. There was not enough vitality in her to shine through the dusty hair and eyes, to animate her any more. She lay in bed most days. Pushpa cleaned out her bedpans. Kalai could not stand the smell. She would never become like that, she promised herself. She paid Anju short, painful visits once a month, flanked by Ilango and Selvi for moral support. With her shaking, liver-spotted hands, Anju thrust damp biscuits on to Kalai, which she had hoarded under her pillow. There were ants. The smells of piss and shit. Kalai would not be responsible. Ganesh was the son. It was his duty to care for the mother. A daughter's duty was to the in-laws. Kalai had no in-laws any more, so she was free. In any case, her duty now was with the Tamil people.

~

Kalai sat at her desk, a pile of paperwork in front of her. She had a pen in her hand, poised over a document. She had to read, then sign. But her eyes were on the window. Dusk had fallen. The breeze rustled through the trees in the garden. Leaves dropped on to the manicured lawn. It was very nice to have a garden, she thought. If she had a little more time, she would spend it in the garden. Could she make time for the garden every day? Perhaps at dawn, so she could see the light breaking over the trees and leaves, smell the freshness of the dew. But at dawn, she would already be preoccupied with thoughts of work. At dawn, she was already at her desk.

That morning, for example. All those orders to sign, which only needed a cursory glance. Then the pile she wanted to give a proper look. Then, notes for the assembly. She hated it. The previous afternoon, when a session ended, her voice had been hoarse, and her ears were ringing. And they hadn't achieved a single thing. Just point-scoring. Mudslinging. Wallowing in useless debate like buffaloes in a mud pond. Sometimes she felt a dictatorship would be a better thing for people such as them. Her people. Parliamentary democracy was for intelligent people willing to have coherent debate that led to rational decision-making. But party politics was impossible. Forever at the brink of an election, forever fearful of losing it. There were the Lok Sabha elections, then the state assembly elections, all the by-elections and, to top it all, talk of an elected mayor for the city. She would be campaigning all the time, instead of ruling. Then there was the headache of the Speechwriter's television channel. She had to do something about that. Oh, but it would be nice to have time to sit in the garden, take a turn, once a day. Maybe she could do it at five-thirty every day, at sunset. But when she did have a rare evening free, well, she never did, it was Selvi who forced her to ...

There she was. Selvi. She came in and said, 'I brought my nephew. Will you meet him? He is a great fan.'

Kalai said, 'Sit for a minute. I've been thinking something.'

Selvi sat down.

'I don't know why I have become CM. It was never my ambition to do so.'

'You have been working too hard.'

'I should be enjoying it, shouldn't I? If this is what I wanted, I should enjoy everything about it. Instead, it feels tedious. Do I care enough about the people? Maybe someone else should do the job, one who is capable of caring more.'

Selvi laughed. 'You think the Speechwriter cares about the people? There isn't a single politician who cares. That is mere fantasy. Gone with the days of the British rule and

Gandhi Congress. You are in it because you were meant for it, and there isn't anyone who can do a better job, a more selfless job.'

'You really think so?' Kalai felt better. Everyone else was worse than her.

'You are feeling depressed because you have been working too hard. Come and meet my nephew. He is a sweet boy. Then we will go shopping. It will take your mind off things. You don't dislike your job. You are just tired.'

~

The boy stole her heart the second she laid eyes on him. He leapt from the sofa and his face flowered into a brilliant, self-conscious grin. How old was he? Fourteen? Thirteen? Such innocence. On the cusp of adulthood. She herself had been, what, fifteen, sixteen, when she was put to work? The boy. Pure as milk. His wavy black hair spilled over his forehead. His eyes sparkled. He wore a neat striped shirt tucked into formal trousers with a belt. He would have dressed carefully to meet her. She wanted to crush him to her. Could he not be her son? He was the kind of boy they would have produced, she and Shekar.

He said, 'Thank you for meeting me. It has been my dream to get your autograph.'

'Sit awhile,' she said. She signed a maxi picture of herself in a Queen Victoria costume, perched unmoving on a throne. From her first PKB movie.

The boy thanked her.

'Tell me about yourself.'

The boy talked. Selvi sat with them, beaming with pride. In truth, Kalai felt a little jealous. He spoke sweetly about his school, his studies, his ambition to be a fighter pilot. Just like Rajiv Gandhi.

Selvi kept a proprietary hand on his shoulder as he answered Kalai's questions, but the boy only had eyes for her. Kalai realised that she was wrong about him being the spitting image of Shekar. An illusion created by the sweep of his hair. The boy had completely different mannerisms. He was darker. He was shorter. His cheekbones were different.

Kalai liked herself as she was reflected in the boy's eyes. He saw her as superhuman. He worshipped her, considered himself blessed to be in her presence. What must he think of Selvi, she who'd made this meeting possible for him? Selvi the priest, a privileged brahmin with a straight line to the gods.

'I like to play chess,' he said. She had asked him what his hobbies were.

'Shall we have a game?' she said.

Selvi nodded enthusiastically.

'You can go shopping,' said Kalai. 'I have not played chess in years. Bring the set.'

Selvi got up and went to find the chess set. Kalai could not remember the last time she had met and spoken intimately with someone his age. Probably when she herself was young, in school. She had not met innocence since she stepped into the wider world to make a living for her mother.

He ran out of things to say, sat with his head bowed. They were waiting for Selvi to appear with the chessboard. Something in her gave with a sigh, softened and enlarged in his presence. With Selvi, she was merely herself, relaxed. With the boy, she felt better than she was. She felt bigger than she was. Cinemascopic.

~

Very early the next morning, Vijayan brought her the news of the dead boy. She had risen, ignored the day's agenda sheet, the piles of files and notes on meetings and proposals on her desk, and stepped out through the patio door into the garden, her eyes on the eastern sky, watching for the pink-yellow dawn. She had not taken two steps down the path through the flowerbeds before her secretary, who lived at the house, appeared. He stood shuffling his feet. She stilled the urge to fire him on the spot.

'What is it, Vijayan?'

'I've been waiting for you to wake, madam, in order to bring you the news.'

'Can it not wait?'

The sun was lifting. The dew would disappear in seconds.

'Of course, madam.'

He still stood there, like a buffalo.

'Tell me.'

'There was this boy, madam, coolie's son, I think, from one of the Indira Nagar slums. On the border of the military compound.'

Her chest constricted. 'Go on.'

'There is a mango tree in the compound, madam. Near the perimeter fence. It should have been electrified. But it wasn't.'

'And?'

'The boy, yesterday, mid–late afternoon, or evening, got on the wall somehow, even with all the barbed wire, and tried to climb the tree. To steal mangoes, is our assumption, madam.'

'And he fell down?' Let it be something silly like that. She could shout at the secretary and be done with it.

'A guard shot him. The bullet entered the head. He fell from the tree, but was still alive. It was a good hour before they got him to the hospital. He died two hours ago.'

Kalai made to sit down, but there was no chair.

'How old is the boy?'

'Thirteen, fourteen.'

Selvi's nephew immediately came to mind. It wasn't him, of course. It was some poor coolie's son.

She went in and sat at her desk. The secretary had asked for permission to draft a statement, but she said she'd do it herself. It was her responsibility. She was in charge. In charge of law and order, in charge of the well-being of the people, especially the poor and the voiceless. She had let them down.

The paper was unbearably crisp. How does one console the parents of a dead child? If she hadn't met Selvi's nephew yesterday, she would not be so affected. Shekar's image filled her mind, lying in rags under a tree with a hole in his skull, dark blood leaking out. All she could think of was Shekar, lying there dead. Why, ten years later, did she mourn her dead husband as though she was a new widow?

She wrote. *I cannot pretend to know what it feels like to have a son and lose him in this nightmarish, tragic way.* She wrote in English. She would ask Vijayan to translate later.

I cannot pretend I can find the right words to comfort you. All I can say is, my prayers are with you, I grieve for your son (insert name) most deeply, and I will do everything in my power to punish those responsible for his death.

She put the pen down. Writing didn't lighten her horror at what had happened under her watch. And she knew these words would never reach the press. She had been chief minister now, for what, one month, nearly two? She already knew how press statements were drafted. Her raw, personal statement was unpalatable. The secretary would draft the statement. He would talk about how the PFD government tried its level best to save the boy. On the Honourable Chief Minister's express orders, top medical experts were summoned. In spite of the PFD government's best efforts, the boy died. The Honourable Chief Minister would make sure that appropriate action was taken on those responsible for such a/an grievous/unforgivable/ unpardonable act. The soldier could have easily discerned it was a harmless boy in the tree. Instead, he chose to shoot. A letter will be written to his commanding officer to hand him over to the Tamil Nadu police for their investigation. All efforts would be made to find justice for the boy. The Honourable Chief Minister's prayers were not with the family, because the PFD, like the JFD and the Dravidas, is an atheist party. Hence the Honourable Chief Minister, in true political style, extends her deepest sympathies and condolences to the parents of the dead boy (insert name), and they could do their own praying.

Outside the window, the sun was way up in the sky. The fresh pastel dawn had faded unnoticed, and now the air hardened. The sunshine reflected off leaves and buildings like steel on steel.

~

'First, madam,' said Vijayan, 'at eight o'clock, we have the honourable central minister for transport coming to pay his respects.' He paused, pushed back the spectacles which had slid down to the tip of his sweaty nose and made a surreptitious attempt to wipe his hand on his trousers before continuing.

'At fifteen minutes past eight, madam, the esteemed chairman of Tata Motors will be paying his respects to you.'

Respects, thought Kalai, standing at the windows, enjoying the last of the cool breezes, was another way to say fear. Tata Motors, she knew, was setting up a new plant fifty miles from the city, to produce some kind of minicar, even smaller than the Maruti 800. How could anything be smaller than the 800? She still had the car, stowed away in one of the back buildings. Ilango took it out for a drive once a week. Just to keep its heart pumping. Of course, cars did not have hearts. But the little red Maruti seemed quite alive to her, and like a friend. The Bentley, for example, was more like an imperious aristocrat. She supposed the Bentley was more suited to someone of her status. She was someone who could squash a big motor company boss's ambitions.

'At nine o'clock, madam, the right honourable His Excellency the Ambassador of Iceland will come to pay his respects.'

'Are they all coming to pay their respects today?'

'Yes, madam, till six o'clock.'

'Then why don't you leave out the bit about paying respects every time you mention a new name, and while you are at it, leave out the prefixes as well, the right honourable, the esteemed, and so on. And yes, you can leave out the madam as well. Then this process will go much faster.'

Vijayan stood, paralysed with indecision, or fear, for a second or two. His grey hair seemed to be standing on end. He was touching fifty. He had been PKB's secretary for ten years. Surely PKB hadn't tolerated this nonsense from him every single day. She won't have it. She would be more efficient. She would save time.

In a strangled voice, with much confusion, he read out, scoring on the paper with his pen as he did, 'At twenty past nine, the new Chief of Police will . . . come.'

Yes, she would make them more efficient. She would whip the beast of government bureaucracy into shape. The breeze was beginning to get warmer.

When he finally finished reading out the day's list of meetings, she said, 'I have nothing scheduled after twenty past six?'

A hope. Like a little limping butterfly, fluttered across her vision. Lie in. Rasam and rice meal. A half-read novel.

Vijayan furiously searched the sheets of paper he held. Then he looked up with wide eyes and, in a strangled voice, bleated, 'Sorry, madam, I missed it. There is a state department banquet at Connemara hotel from seven till ten, and there is an urgent private meeting requested by the personal secretary to the Karnataka CM, over the water issue, which we could only schedule at ten o'clock, in the meeting room of the hotel itself.'

The butterfly faded right away. She was inured to nature's charms. The day breaking outside held no attraction to one such as her.

'What time is it?'

'Five forty-five, madam.'

'Come,' she said, walking back to her chair behind the desk, and taking out her green pen. 'Let us see if we can make a list of government departments to inspect before the first honourable fellow turns up to pay his respects to madam.'

~

Kalai watched from the sofa while Selvi stood in front of the mirror, mesmerised. She was decked out like a goddess. They both were. This was Selvi's idea of relaxing on a free evening with Kalai. They looked like fat twins, she thought, with a trace of disgust at herself and at Selvi. It was not something she'd ever get used to enjoying, child of austerity that she was. All this preoccupation with jewels and saris and display. She did not need so much. Every time the accountant wanted to go over the accounts, or the lawyer wanted to draw up the will, or this or that, she found excuses to put them off. It was embarrassing to discuss wealth with anyone, let alone male strangers. In any case, she had no dependants. She didn't care who got how much after her death. They could all speculate and be disappointed. She would be happier dying a pauper. Perhaps she could give everything away to some charity. She should summon the lawyer. Or just tell him on the phone. Or have the secretary instruct him.

'I will return this,' said Selvi, indicating her heavy gold-threaded sari in pink and green. 'I will get us another design. The mango shapes are too big.'

Kalai's sari was of exactly the same design, although in blue and brown. At moments like this Kalai didn't understand Selvi at all. Herself, she found it tiresome to shop for clothes and jewellery. And to have the energy to go shopping all over again, on a whim, discarding something she had spent ages choosing. Did she take her husband along for these things? Varadan. That shifty little man. After all, he must be paying the bills. Or did he simply give her a joint bank account or wads of cash or a credit card? She herself didn't have a credit card. She did not have to deal with money, or pay for things. She knew that nowadays everyone was using credit cards. Everyone, except, of course, the poor. That majority population whom she only ever saw on election campaigns, or while distributing free stuff.

'Will you be able to come? There is a splendid new sari shop on Usman Road.'

'No. I can't imagine what people would say. CM goes sari shopping.'

But really, public opinion was just an excuse. Why would people have a problem with the CM choosing her own saris, in any case? They would be delighted. It would make her more like them, more human. No, it was just an excuse to slip out of the monotony of having to choose saris. Ostensibly, Selvi was picking saris for their birthdays. She had insisted they try them out. It was fun, the dressing up, the adorning of each other with jewels, perfumes. She had never had that when she was younger. Not for herself, not for fun. She had been draped in hundreds of costumes, but it was all for the hero and the movie audience. Never for herself. And this, what Selvi was doing, was for herself.

'I am sure your judgement is sufficient to choose saris for the both of us,' said Kalai, and Selvi smiled. An odd look, like that of triumph, passed over her features. Selvi always looked radiant when trying on new things. Their birthdays fell within a week of each other. Selvi had got it into her head that they would celebrate their birthdays on the same day, give a party to close family and friends. No politicians, nobody official. Kalai had thought, why not. Why not fill the house with children and spouses and aunties and babies, for a change, instead of drab, bitter, sycophantic politicians? But it had to be all Selvi's relatives. Kalai would not invite a single one of hers. Where were they when Anju was impoverished and didn't have a paisa to call her own? Even her own brother Ganesh she didn't speak to nowadays. He still was in Delhi, she supposed.

Selvi was saying, 'I am making a list of people to invite, although you know it will be impossible to stick to it.'

'Call who you like,' said Kalai.

Of course, she couldn't tell Selvi not to call her husband. Selvi knew Kalai didn't like him much, although Kalai had never said a word. She had only met him, briefly, twice. Bald, skinny, short, with a pot belly. But it wasn't his looks that bothered her. He looked like a movie hero compared to some of her ministers. No, there was something about him. Was it his super-whites? He wasn't a politician, so why was he always in spotless white from top to toe? He called himself a businessman, but was unspecific about his interests. And what was with his eyes? He was always wearing shaded glasses. She had never seen his eyes. There was something a bit jumpy about him, just underneath his skin. She could sense it. It could be that he was merely nervous. He didn't have his wife's confidence, her elan, wafting in and out of the CM's house like she owned it, unimpressed by what leaders of the world she bumped into while bringing a trinket or two for her friend from a newly opened shop. She was always bringing Kalai presents. As though they were a couple in an English movie.

'I will not wear so many jewels, I think,' said Kalai. Already, one of the necklaces was biting into the back of her neck.

Selvi turned around, beaming. 'I have a great idea,' she said. 'We should get a photographer, and take pictures together. Like sisters. Oh, I know just the one, has a studio on Paramount Road. He did my cousin's wedding. He is very good. I will ring him tomorrow.'

Kalai let herself be carried away by Selvi's enthusiasm. An old fad. All the teenage girls in school had a photograph of themselves, in front of the mirror so you could see their front and back. Silk sari, jewels, ornaments, elaborate head decorations and flowers twirled all the way around their long, plaited hair. She had never taken such a photo when she was thirteen or fourteen, stepping into womanhood, a photo to capture her own seduction of herself in the mirror. They had been too poor. Anju had refused. Anju had used the harshest words Kalai had ever heard in her life. Sell your body, she had said. Was that it? We will have to sell your body to pay for such a thing. Kalai hadn't even understood what Anju meant, till some months passed, and the knowledge slipped into her through some mysterious osmosis.

'Get who you like,' she said to Selvi. 'We will have a grand party. What is the point of money if you cannot spend it?'

~

Three hundred housewives, not in their best silk saris, but in their good saris, fairly new polyester ones, bought for last year's Pongal or Deepavali, or gifted to them by their mistress in return for a long year's housework, stood queuing patiently to receive their ration cards from her.

Kalai stood on the stage, trying to ignore her legs, which felt like pillars or elephant legs. She had to keep blinking, for her eyes swam with exhaustion. A feeling of mild nausea kept her in a bubble in the midst of the noisome event. The launch of the new ration card for the poor, which promised them a kilo of rice for one rupee every week, a kilo of lentils for two rupees, a litre of palm oil for three rupees. Somebody in the cabinet meeting earlier had suggested it ought to be called the one–two–three scheme.

The meeting had lasted all day, and achieved little, which was the reason for her exhaustion. She had rejected the silly idea, and had named it the 'Revival Scheme'. After all, she was merely carrying on what was started by Ayya, continued by PKB, and even the Speechwriter. She couldn't claim ownership of someone else's scheme. But she had to make a scene of it, an event of it, or people wouldn't notice. It would seem that without the fanfare and the chest-thumping, she wasn't serious, that she was a mere dabbler. Or worse, if she didn't make so much noise, she would get lost in the clamour everybody else was making. She would be forgotten and swept aside by the relentless push of time. There was the re-election to consider.

At the lectern, a white-clad on the microphone introduced the scheme and used the opportunity to sing Kalai's praises as though she had invented fire itself for humanity. He praised the great dead men of the party, Ayya and PKB, for a long hour, although Ayya had technically started the Dravidas party. He also slammed the opposition, the Speechwriter and his ambitious nephews and sons.

Her head threatened to separate into two. Kalai wondered if it would be appropriate for her to be seen rolling her neck. Very close to the stage, to the left, there was every single local television channel with a camera. Including hers. KA TV. And seated and scribbling furiously were the print journalists. Dancing around like monkeys were the photographers. She had to remain seated, remain still, with a slight smile of benevolence pasted on her face. All day at the cabinet meeting, she had been under a barrage of male opinions. They were discussing the water crisis. She hadn't received any useful suggestions. She would speak with the civil service tomorrow. They were educated. They did not have any political agenda. Some of them actually wanted to serve the people.

At the meeting, they had also discussed the coming central government elections, and a campaign schedule had been totted up for allies. The party's new ambition was to have a role in the central government. Have a piece of that pie. It would be wonderful, she thought, as the speaker began quoting from a PKB movie, her headache deserting her just for a second as a thrill went through her body. If a PFD minister could become a central minister with an important portfolio, like education, or railways. Yes, there was a chance now, since the Congress wasn't winning easy majorities any more, and the northern states were coming to be dominated by regional parties as well. Yes, anything could happen.

The introduction ended. The patient housewives still waited patiently. The minister for food and welfare now started his speech. He slurred a little. His eyes looked red in the stage spotlights. Had he been drinking? In the daytime? And theirs was the party that abolished toddy and lottery tickets. Anger swept through her. She trembled, struggled to bring herself under control. It was the exhaustion that made it so difficult to control her emotions. An MP, slurring drunk at a public event, in front of the chief minister herself. She would fire him right after the event.

He raised his arm, raised his voice, in rhetoric. 'Our benevolent leader, our mother, our head of family . . .'

She frowned. All this was a bit unnecessary. The man was a couple of years older than her. He was calling her the party's mother. The people's mother. She was only forty-five. It was like a physical assault when they suggested such a thing. It was a violation. But what could she do, except act stern, act, well, like a mother, like a benevolent matriarch, when it happened? They seemed so reverent in her presence, bowing and scraping. She was only forty-five. And these men, averaging sixty, kowtowing to her.

As tiring as the job itself were the obsequies she inspired in these people. All day at the cabinet meeting. Respectful this, honourable that. Even in their own private meeting. She had to order them not to waste time with the appendages and platitudes. But how could she order them to change their body language? To stop crooking their shoulders, to stop covering their mouths, to stop bending their backs as though carrying sacks of rice?

What woman had to go through with this? There was

the holy woman in Kerala, the Mother. Sonia Gandhi no one called mother. There was Avvaiyar. Did she ever exist? Asking for a boon to be turned into a sixty-year-old grandee when she was sixteen, so she didn't have to be family-bound. Did she gain posture and composure just as easily as she swapped pimples for wrinkles? Did it come naturally to Avvaiyar to look smug and deserving when old men with dodgy knees hobbled up and down and bent low to show their respect to her?

She looked down at her feet for a moment. They still tingled. Just yesterday, someone had tried to fall at her feet. She had forgotten propriety and seized him by the shoulders, but just for an instant. Thankfully there were no photographers nearby, or it would have looked like an embrace. She could not let this sort of thing happen. She was not Avvaiyar. She was not sixty years old.

Her eyes swept the seated (hundreds?) people. All the press were gathered, all the leaders, ministers. Select public – the rich who had donated enough to be deserving of a darshan. She made a face at her own slip. She was just thinking she must put a stop to all the sycophancy, and already she was casting herself in the role of a goddess. She ought to remember that it was her position, the power she held through occupying the post of chief minister, that made these people bend backwards to please her, fete her. Without that, she was nothing. If they got a chance, they would trample her into the dust. Her enemies only waited for a chance to humiliate her. How could she forget Maran?

She touched her waist, making sure, feeling the comfort that was the vest, and the coat that kept the loose end of her sari tucked away.

Finally, she was on her feet, handing out the hundred new ration cards. Humble housewives, who didn't meet her eyes, delicately plucked the card from her hand and scurried away, as if they were ants scurrying from fire. Wait, she wanted to tell them. Smile back at me. Meet eyes, linger, ask after my health as you would your sister. But these were the downtrodden. These women had no say even in the running of their own lives, their reproductive systems, the length of their hair and how they wore it. And much as they tolerated her for having been loved by one such as PKB, they were horrified by her. She was an anomaly in their midst. She was a woman who belied her gender.

Breaths of relief rose up in the air and people shuffled to their feet. The cameras were being shoved back into cases. Kalai thought longingly of bed, quiet, a dark room. She turned to leave, deciding she wouldn't brook anyone barring her way home with yet more sycophancy. She could see a group of white-clad hovering at the end of the stage. She took a step away when a cry, like that of a pained calf, emerged from behind her. Reluctantly, she turned. The cameras were flashing again. The silence in the hall was abuzz with static.

'My mother, my queen,' the man was crying, fully prostrate on the floor. She could only see his back, his head, and his sandalled feet sticking out of the end of his veshti, his hairy arms, fingertips an inch away from her feet.

She parted lips to speak, then froze. She realised who he was.

A bunch of white-clad, her own party men, men who did things for her, things that were necessary, stood in the corner of the stage.

They looked smug and pleased with themselves, like the dogs in movies that brought back the ball which their owners threw in some paradise-like setting, a green and grassy field. The dogs with their coats glowing, eyes shining with health and adoration, standing, begging for a pat on the head. They had delivered Maran to her, suitably contrite, chewed up a little around the edges, and now they would expect a reward.

'Forgive your son,' cried Maran. She continued standing. Let him grovel at her feet. She stood, larger than herself. An image on a movie screen. Unmoved as a goddess in a temple.

2005

Officer Chandramohan stepped down from his police jeep, stumbled in his nervousness. He put a shaky hand on the jeep rail to steady himself. The sight that awaited him did nothing to ease his nerves. His sphincter muscles loosened. Dear god, Muruga, Shanmuga, he prayed. Let me not soil myself in front of the entire country's news media. He had hardly taken a step towards the house, flanked by his fellow officers – although none of them were useless fellows, he was the one entrusted with this specific task, he was the one in the firing line – when the bulbs started flashing, microphones thrust into his face and questions fell on him like rubble from the backs of lorries.

He had already emptied his bowels four times that morning. Even his wife was so nervous she'd vomited. The previous night, he had been summoned at an ungodly hour to the presence, the personal, private presence, of the newly sworn-in Chief Minister. Chandramohan had received his orders. His bowel trouble had started even before he left the CM's sprawling house in R. Nagar.

The raid party was already in the house. When Chandramohan walked in, they were dragging items from cupboards, piling them neatly in the middle of the hall. The furniture had been moved already to the corners. There didn't seem to be anyone from the house in sight. He tried to pick out who was in charge. They all wore safari suits. Men from the Central Bureau of Investigation. Just as a CBI man caught his eye, another walked into his vision carrying a pile of jewellery cases. He wore JFD party colours.

'Hey you,' called Chandramohan. 'Who let you in?'

'Aahn?' said the man, rather with insouciance. Chandramohan immediately panicked. He'd been in this godforsaken city more than a year. He seemed never to get it right. Who to pick on. Who not to pick on. The man in JFD colours ignored Chandramohan and went to lay the pile of leather cases on a stool. He then started opening them one by one and laying them on the floor as though he were working on the display window in a jewellery store. He nodded to someone at the door. Three men with cameras rushed in and began filming the goods on display. Chandramohan had time to notice the logos on the sides of the cameras, before he was addressed by the safari suit who'd first caught his eye.

'Best let them get on with it,' said the man in a kind tone, the sandalwood paste between his eyebrows crinkling.

'Are you in charge?'

'Yes, of the raid. I suppose you've come for the arrest.'

'Will you come with me?'

The man considered. 'Yes, but I will stand behind you, won't say a word. Who knows how things will turn around in five years' time.'

'You think there is a chance?' Chandramohan's belly did another flip. His wife. His family. His career.

The CBI officer looked sympathetic. He was homegrown.

He knew how things were in this godforsaken state controlled by movie stars and speechwriters.

'Listen,' he told Chandramohan. 'Every five years there is a political landslide. The people are completely predictable, and also completely unpredictable. Look at all the media, rooting for her downfall. You read the papers, you think the public opinion is one thing. You go to the villages, it is another. Come and have lunch with me one day. I sympathise with your situation, but I cannot help you. I have a family too. Never mind five years from now. Even tomorrow is unpredictable in this political climate. Learn to improve your Tamil. It will help you in your job.'

Chandramohan nodded reluctantly. Every godforsaken Tamil was full of opinions. 'Where is she?'

'In her bedroom. Alone. Come, let us get it done with.'

They climbed the stairs, the CBI man leading. But then without warning, he stopped midway and awkwardly shuffled his bulk to one side. He gestured to Chandramohan to go ahead.

'I will stand behind you, by the door. I do not want to have her think it was my idea, you understand.'

'Aren't you paranoid? She knows it is not us acting of our own accord.'

'Nevertheless,' said the CBI man, still eerily cheerful.

Chandramohan hadn't thought to ask his name. He had the feeling the man would refuse to tell him.

'She is a very smart woman, but unpredictable. She might take it personally, or she might see reason. Why take chances?'

Chandramohan held tight his sphincter, breathed like a marathon runner on the short walk from landing to bedroom. He had no need to knock. It was open. Inside, by the window, a suitcase next to her, stood Madam Kalai Arasi herself. In the flesh.

Chandramohan stepped forward, stepped back. The sides of his throat seemed glued together. Try as he might, he could not get a single word out. His mind went blank. He stood with his mouth gaping like a landed guppy.

The freshly dethroned ex-CM turned, looked him up and down, expressionless. 'Come, inspector,' she said, not unkindly. 'Let us go.' Then she swept past him and out of the room, leaving Chandramohan to pick up her suitcase. The CBI man was nowhere to be seen.

~

At the sound of knocking, Kalai turned from the small metal chair at the slab of cement that constituted her desk. The jailer shifted his feet at the door. Men were always standing in doorways, shuffling their feet. The door was not locked in an A-class prison. For the rich and the powerful. She hadn't known when she was brought here that there were such things. All she had known of jails came from the movies. Filthy, full of bunks and men, murder and mayhem. This was more luxurious than many of the portions she had lived in with Anju through her childhood.

'Visitor, madam.'

'Bring her.'

Who could it be? One of the small pleasures of being in jail was the daily visit. She never liked to ask who it was, before they were brought to her. It was pleasant to speculate, to enjoy the suspense, to savour it like a piece of jaggery.

The room measured twelve feet by ten. It had a single bed and a thin mattress. She could bring her own pillow and sheets. In fact, when she arrived, a new set of bedding had been waiting for her. She never did find out who had been so thoughtful. Perhaps the jailer himself. There was a small steel chair, which had been impossible to sit on, but after a week, it seemed the height of comfort. The body adjusted to everything. What had been indispensable a week before became quickly superfluous. What did she need other than a change of clothes, simple food and her thoughts? The desk was a cement slab projecting from a corner of the wall. She liked to sit in her chair and stare intently at the surface of the desk. So plain, yet so complex, the greys and whites, the abstract patterns in the cement. It helped to heal the mind. She felt as though she was recovering from a long illness.

A tinkly sound at the door. Kalai looked up, expecting Selvi to be standing there. She would always associate tinkly sounds with Selvi, all that jewellery she liked to wear. But no one was there. It would take a good while for the jailer to negotiate the long corridors and locked doors, before he would find her guest and fetch her back here. As a privileged A-class jailbird, she could meet visitors in her own room. The cattle class had to huddle in the damp, shabby visitor rooms. At least she assumed they were damp and shabby, possibly with the smell of urine too, although she had never been in one. Even here, in the corridors of the A class, there was the whiff of it. It seemed as though in all great institutional buildings the fabric of the buildings themselves, the fabric of history itself, was imbued with the pungent stink of urine. It went to show something, didn't it? If she had a bit more education, she would know what it showed.

She got up and paced. She wished Selvi would come. One whole week with no word from her. Who was Kalai fooling? Selvi would stand by her husband and her various male relatives involved in the dozens of scams the other party seemed to be unearthing. Selvi was busy, with the complications, the police enquiries, whatnot. Maybe they had arrested Selvi, and were not telling her. It was impossible for Kalai to believe Selvi would have actively been against her, in any way. It had been no more than foolishness on the part of the two of them. Playing at pyjama parties. Playing shopping-shopping.

How all the gifts and trinkets had accumulated, over ten years. Kalai had never asked where the money came from, was never told. Did Selvi choose not to know? Like Kalai chose not to. How could she, she who had always viewed with awe the way wealthy people wore and breathed wealth? It was Pinky's family she had wanted for herself, the richest family she knew in her youth. In her old age, she had acquired a longed-for sister, a sister who indulged her with gifts, who had money like Pinky. Her husband was in real estate, just like Pinky's father had been. Of course, Kalai had her suspicions. She was not foolish. When she had met Selvi, she dressed modestly, ran a video shop, was thin. Ten years later, she wore diamonds and the best silk. She had become fat.

Kalai put a hand on the wall, felt the damp, flaky surface. Just because she herself did not actively pursue wealth, did not spend, nor even carry money, she had thought herself above everything. Her humble origins had made her, somehow, afraid to dwell too much on the sources of wealth. After all, a part of her knew that, in a country like India, all wealth was dirty at source. In fact, wealth, by definition, was made at somebody's or something's expense.

Refusing to deal with lawyers, or making a will, did not stop the wealth from accumulating in her own coffers. The charges read out to her had seemed incredible. That cannot be me, she had thought. They were talking about some greedy woman. Lists and lists, of jewellery, saris, shoes, vehicles, buildings, land, houses, even a strip of beachfront development. Shares in teak forests for goodness' sake. All in proxy names, Selvi's, her husband's, her adopted son's – what was his name? And more shamefully, in her own name. All these years, she had told her lawyers to sort all her money matters themselves. Don't trouble me with details. Just show me where to sign.

She sat on the bed, then got up again. Nobody would now believe that she had never been interested in wealth, in possessions. Nobody. Her own mother, if she were alive, would not believe her. Anju had always been ready to think the worst of her. Ninety-nine fellows could come and tell Anju that Kalai was a good girl. But when the hundredth came and told her Kalai was the devil, Anju would say, 'I always had the suspicion. Now you have confirmed it.'

How was she to counterclaim against all the parading and peacocking and mudslinging in the Speechwriter's papers and TV channels? How could she, stuck here in jail, prove she was a decent woman, a good leader who had done her best? Was it time to quit politics, and retire to some hill station? A part of her immediately eased at such a thought. The question . . .

It was Ilango, after all. He shuffled in, sat down wearily on the chair. He looked the same as he did forty years ago. Scrawny, not too much grey in his hair, no sign of balding. The poor: their only blessing was that they were too busy making ends meet to give a thought to how ugly they looked. The rich had all the luxury of time.

Kalai did not want to sit down. She paced. Suddenly she was a jungle cat, prowling, plotting. What was it about Ilango that his presence fed her vitality? He still had not said a word. He was just watching her, with an equanimous expression. He was her brother, her father, even a part of herself.

'Did you see Selvi?' she asked him. No need for smoke and mirrors with Ilango.

'I gave her a good talking-to,' he said. 'She will stand by you, even if she has to go against her husband. She will not turn approver against you. On pain of death even.'

Kalai was surprised. 'Will she? It is her own husband.'

Ilango shrugged.

Her best friend had not forsaken her.

'I have been thinking about the future,' she said.

'Second innings.' Ilango grinned.

'To start with, no more jewellery or silk saris.'

'Yes.'

Kalai felt thinner than she had in years. Her blouse hung off her arms. All this pacing about the room, all the thinking, the jail food, disgusting as it was. She felt hungry, probably for the first time in years. Ravenous.

As if reading her mind, Ilango handed her a plastic bag. There was a box inside. Some oil had seeped through the cardboard. It smelled spicy, clean, nutritious.

'Selvi sent this. She made it herself. She wants to know if she can visit you tomorrow.'

Kalai opened the box, dug out the spoon.

'No more vest and coat,' said Kalai. 'No more Black Cat security.'

The food was delicious. She did not need men and steel to feel safe any more. She was invincible in her very core.

'Five years,' said Ilango. 'Five years and then there will be a landslide.'

~

Kanmani switched off the television in the middle of *Little Family*'s end credits. Her favourite soap. She pushed the remote under her left thigh where it relieved some of the pain in her gluteus. The clock struck nine. The tube light sizzled as though sympathising with her about the weather. So late, and still so sultry. She couldn't open the windows. The mosquitoes would swarm in. Her husband away in

Pune. No one to wait on in the evenings for three more days. She'd already had her rasam and rice. When one had to cook for herself, the appetite went away. She could phone her daughter, who was in Manipal for her studies. But they had only spoken the day before. Again the pain came into her belly, the loss of her second child. They should have tried again. A younger one would now be lying on the bed, reading his storybooks or playing on his computer. She could take him a glass of milk, tell him off for making a mess with his cricket shoes in the puja room. But there was no one. Two minutes past nine o'clock.

To escape from her own thoughts, she switched on the television once more. The news. She sat up straighter. A long lens shot of Kalai Arasi coming out of prison. How long was she in for? Three weeks? A month? Lost weight. Where was all her jewellery? No coat or vest. Plain and simple. Glowing with health. Elegant lady. Kalai Arasi smiled demurely. Raised two fingers. Put her hands together, thanked the public for their support. Selvi appeared. Kanmani leaned forward in surprise. Selvi flung herself at Kalai Arasi's feet. Then they embraced. What was the newsreader saying? She turned up the volume.

'. . . has turned state's witness and given evidence leading to her husband being apprehended and charged with engineering the scams Kalai Arasi was originally charged with. In a statement, the respected Chief Minister condemned Mrs Selvi for giving in to threats and undue pressure, and setting a bad example to womanhood for turning against her own husband . . .'

Kanmani guffawed. The CM should listen to himself to hear how ridiculous he sounded. This was the problem with her favourite channel being owned by the Speechwriter's family. Such biased news. If it were not for *Little Family* she wouldn't watch it at all.

She rooted out the remote and switched channels. KA TV. PKB's handsome face filled the screen. Every evening, they played PKB's songs. He was dancing on a table in a palatial house. The master of the house glowered. His daughters milled about, coveting PKB. The servants of the house swayed in ecstasy in a corner. PKB sang, 'I am not a king and this is not my rule. A poor man may be poor, but he is not a fool.'

For all that song, he ruled for thirteen years. And now the Speechwriter's rule, and the streets full of Tata Estates and Sumos with blackened windows, the flag on the bonnet, going very fast. His sons and nephews, their cousins, goondas. Thugs, plaguing the streets. PFD and JFD. Kanmani shook her head. Every five years, the Tamil people swapped the grindstone for the millstone and vice versa.

On election day, her husband had been late from work. For hours she had waited, and while waiting, she had debated whom to vote for. She rang her husband, but he was busy-busy. Getting impatient, looking at the clock, she was about to start walking by herself, when he came. She had jumped in the car, and they managed to reach the polling station just as it was about to close. She still hadn't decided. For a whole minute, her pen had hovered above the two options, before, just for a change, she had voted for

JFD. When she came out and asked her husband, to her surprise, he had voted JFD too. Now, of course, already, the change had soured.

Kanmani did not drive a car. She relied on the bus service to go visiting. If she had a job, she could have had a car. Even a dhobi job required a college degree nowadays. She should have had a degree. Her condition, when she married, had been that she would be allowed to pursue a degree course in Madras. Neither her in-laws nor her husband kept their promise. The politicians did not keep their promises either. What choice did she have, other than to make do with what she had? Better the devil known . . .

PKB jostled with Kalai Arasi on a pirate ship, singing. Such chemistry. It occurred to Kanmani that there was no one around, the windows were shut, the fans were running loudly to drown out her noises for any nosy neighbour with snake ears. She could sing along. Loudly. As she used to do as a child. On the television screen, PKB swayed with the boat, singing. Kalai swayed with PKB, singing. Kanmani swayed in her sitting room, and sang along with them.

Let us fly like the birds, dance like the waves. Let us sing the song of freedom.

~

Every door, from her cell to the wide metal gates opening on to Kodambakkam High Road, had been unlocked for her passage. Policemen and women, sentries like those in stone outside villages, stood rooted to the spot, in doorways, behind desks, beside chairs, shelves, along corridors. They stared straight ahead, yet she saw the awe, the worship, the fear. She glided past them to freedom.

Flanked by Ilango and Vijayan, devoid of the bulletproof vest, shorn of all jewellery except a single pinpoint diamond in her nostril, nevertheless, she felt herself glow.

Dozens of reporters. Flashing bulbs. She raised her hands together. Beyond the reporters, the people in their hundreds and thousands. A storm of noise. Bodies pierced with hooks, spears. Those who had sacrificed hair, limbs, tongues, for her. Women hollering, ululating. People in black vestments, rose drapes. Her colours. Colours of death and life.

'Arasi! Arasi!' The cries everywhere.

She gazed past the cameras, microphones. She looked to the people. Spoke to them directly. 'Your trust in me has been vindicated. My sole purpose in life is to serve you. I rule only to serve.'

She turned to leave, her silence proof against all the reporters' questions and emotional demonstrations from the diehards. Then Selvi appeared. Dishevelled, hair mussed, in a very plain sari. Like a slain banana tree, she fell at Kalai's feet.

'Sister,' cried Selvi. 'Forgive me, this poor, wretched sinner.'

Kalai helped Selvi up. Embraced her. 'There, there,' she said.

Tears streaked Selvi's face. The vermilion on her hair parting, a sign of her servitude to marriage, smudged with sweat, had run down into her eyebrows. What a grotesque creature she was.

'Find her another car,' Kalai said to Vijayan.

She would forgive the husband for Selvi's sake, but she would never let them close again. Who did she need? No one.

To Ilango, she said, 'Let us go.'

And take it all back. Her crown. Her rule.

She would travel to the party HQ. Manikavel, her stand-in, would formally hand back the mantle. More journalists, more photos.

She pressed a button and the window whispered down. The smell of damp earth. The sky looked heavy. The air charged with an imminent thunderstorm. It was always thus in November.

Tomorrow, battle stations. The Speechwriter and his ruling party best batten down. She would rain fire upon them for the next four years till the general elections.

A twenty-foot-tall cut-out near the Anna Flyover. Her image from ten years ago, with just the second half of her name in big rose letters bordered in black. Arasi. A loudspeaker blared near it. An old film song of hers. 'A girl like cake to rule us. A girl called Arasi to woo us.' PKB using the royal 'we', ironically.

Her name, Kalai Arasi, meant 'she who was ruler of the arts', but PKB simply called her 'Arasi'. To him, she had always been just 'Queen'.

Kalai turned from the window to look past Ilango's shoulder, ahead. The song faded.

And she was that, she thought. She was Queen.

Acknowledgements

I am indebted to **Harry Whitehead**, who has been a most supportive and loving husband, while also meticulously editing three drafts of *The Queen* with matchless understanding, vision and skill.

Thanks also to you **Baby Brân**, for accommodating the edits in your young life, and bringing such joy.

A great deal of thanks I owe **Sabyn Javeri** for being the miracle I needed when I needed it the most.

Kanishka Gupta, wonderful, tireless and kind agent.

R. Sivapriya, for the faith and guts, for intuitive, knowledgeable and immaculate editing, and, erm, for spotting all the booboos.

Corinne Fowler, for sacrificing some of her holiday and reading an early draft.

And finally, **Coral Atkins**, for reading with such enthusiasm and giving such encouragement. I miss you every day and I'm so glad you were part of this book's journey.

A Note on the Author

Anita Sivakumaran's poetry and short fiction have been anthologised in collections published by Bloodaxe and Virago among others. *The Queen* is her first novel.

juggernaut

THE APP FOR INDIAN READERS

Fresh, original books tailored for mobile and for India. Starting at ₹10.

www.juggernaut.in

1

CRAFTED FOR MOBILE READING

Thought you would never read a book on mobile? Let us prove you wrong.

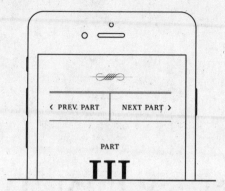

Beautiful Typography

The quality of print transferred
to your mobile. Forget ugly PDFs.

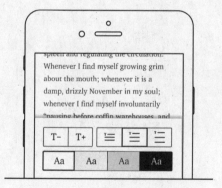

Customizable Reading

Read in the font size, spacing
and background of your liking.

AN EXTENSIVE LIBRARY

Fresh new original Juggernaut books from the likes of Sunny Leone, Twinkle Khanna, Rujuta Diwekar, William Dalrymple, Pankaj Mishra, Arundhati Roy and lots more. Plus, books from partner publishers and all the free classics you want.

3

**DON'T
JUST READ;
INTERACT**

*We're changing the reading experience from
passive to active.*

Ask authors questions

Get all your answers from the horse's mouth.
Juggernaut authors actually reply to every
question they can.

Rate and review

Let everyone know of your favourite reads or
critique the finer points of a book – you will be
heard in a community of like-minded readers.

Gift books to friends

For a book-lover, there's no nicer gift than
a book personally picked. You can even
do it anonymously if you like.

Enjoy new book formats

Discover serials released in parts over
time, picture books including comics,
and story-bundles at discounted rates.

4

LOWEST PRICES & ONE-TAP BUYING

Books start at ₹10 with regular discounts and free previews.

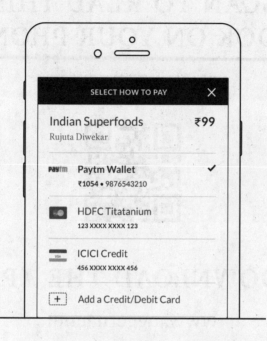

Paytm Wallet, Cards &
Apple Payments.

On Android, just add a Paytm Wallet once and
buy any book with one tap. On iOS, pay with one
tap with your iTunes-linked debit/credit card.

Click the QR Code with a QR scanner app
or type the link into the Internet browser
on your phone to download the app.

SCAN TO READ THIS BOOK ON YOUR PHONE

www.juggernaut.in

DOWNLOAD THE APP

www.juggernaut.in

For our complete catalogue, visit www.juggernaut.in
To submit your book, send a synopsis and two
sample chapters to books@juggernaut.in
For all other queries, write to contact@juggernaut.in